四明
雅韵

宁波古代诗歌英译

POEMS PORTRAYING
CENTURIES-OLD CITY OF NINGBO

汉英对照

编译　辛红娟　张智中

编委　杨　楠　吴红靓　蒋梦缘

绘图　刘芝秀

译审　[美] Crystal Gao

浙江大学出版社
ZHEJIANG UNIVERSITY PRESS
· 杭州

图书在版编目（CIP）数据

四明雅韵：宁波古代诗歌英译：汉英对照 / 辛红
娟，张智中编译. -- 杭州：浙江大学出版社，2023.1
ISBN 978-7-308-23329-3

Ⅰ.①四… Ⅱ.①辛… ②张… Ⅲ.①古典诗歌－诗
集－中国－汉、英 Ⅳ.①I222

中国版本图书馆CIP数据核字(2022)第226150号

四明雅韵——宁波古代诗歌英译（汉英对照）

辛红娟　　张智中　编译

策　　划	包灵灵	
责任编辑	包灵灵	
责任校对	黄静芬	
封面设计	林智广告	
出版发行	浙江大学出版社	
	（杭州市天目山路148号　　邮政编码　310007）	
	（网址：http://www.zjupress.com）	
排　　版	杭州林智广告有限公司	
印　　刷	杭州高腾印务有限公司	
开　　本	880mm×1230mm　1/32	
印　　张	6.25	
字　　数	140千	
版 印 次	2023年1月第1版　2023年1月第1次印刷	
书　　号	ISBN 978-7-308-23329-3	
定　　价	68.00元	

公元 742 年，也就是唐玄宗天宝元年夏，四十二岁的李白告别东鲁（今属山东），携家室来到会稽（今绍兴）游览，和道士吴筠一起隐居剡中（今嵊州）。在此期间，天台山、四明山等传说中的仙山福地都留下了他不倦登临的足迹。四明山由天台发脉向东北行一百三十里，涌为二百八十峰，周围八百余里，最高峰上有四个洞穴，每当天高气清的时候，远远望去，四个洞穴如同四面通透的窗户，又恍若四只澄澈的眼睛，日月星辰之光贯穿其中，所以号为"四明山"，又被称为"四窗"。传说古代神仙登陆往往就选择在此山，这是道教三十六洞天之第九洞天，名曰丹山赤水之天。

如此神奇的风景，如此神秘的传说，怎不令"五岳寻仙不辞远，一生好入名山游"的李白心驰神往！

四明山没有辜负李白的期待。在李白的诗中，四明山绵延"三千里"，日出前红霞万丈，日出时红光散落似绮，映衬着冰雪覆盖的山崖。置身于苍茫天海之间的李白，情不自禁张开双臂向天空高举，全身心拥抱从辉耀的阳光中驰骋而来的青龙车、白虎车，那是来迎接他的仙官。在那一刻，他似乎也和仙人们一起腾云驾车，飘飘然凌空飞去，在浩淼的太虚中傲视尘寰。

李白在四明山的这次惊鸿一瞥堪称古代宁波在诗词中的惊艳亮相："四明三千里，朝起赤城霞。日出红光散，分辉照雪崖。一餐咽琼液，五内发金沙。举手何所待，青龙白虎车。"（李白《早望海霞边》）而命运的安排就是如此奇妙：就在李白登临四明山之后不久，他生命中的"青龙白虎车"真的向他飞驰而来——同年秋，李白等来了唐玄宗的诏命，他随即奔赴长安，"仰天大笑出门去"，真正迎来了他一生中供奉翰林的"高光"时刻。从此，四明山留下的不仅仅是神仙的足迹，更烙印了李白浪漫的诗篇。

宁波古称"四明"，即得名于四明山。对于李白而言，明州的历史并不遥远：唐玄宗开元二十六年（738），越州鄮县置明州，天宝元年（742）改为余姚郡，乾元元年（758）复名为明州，此即宁波的前身。

在古典诗词中，四明山是明州的地标。此地有山有海，亦佛亦仙，有壮美秀丽的自然风景可供人游目骋怀，有绵长丰厚的历史文化可供人沉潜涵泳，有独具特色的风土人情可供人流连忘返，更有或在此生长或在此驻足停留过的人一代一代讲述着属于他们的故事——这一切塑造了一个诗意的明州，一个文化的宁波，一座美貌与才华并存、情意与智慧共生的城市。

为此，宁波应该感谢李白和所有将故事与诗篇镌刻在这里的历史人物，也应该感谢《四明雅韵——宁波古代诗歌英译》的编译者辛红娟教授、张智中教授团队。辛红娟教授并非土生土长的宁波人，然而宁波丰饶的文化源泉显然让她如鱼得水。我和辛红娟教授相识相知已经 20 多年，我们在中南大学共事多年，虽然研究领域不同，联系却非常紧密，她调到宁波大学之后我们的交流不但没有减少，反而更加频繁。我深深了解她是一个在翻译领域深耕多年，且对中国传统文化有着较为全面和深入理解的学者，她的勤奋与严谨更让我由衷敬佩。在《四明雅韵》的编选和翻译过程中，她经常会通过微信和电话与我讨论；我去宁波的时候，她带着团队骨干成员来和我一起交流；有时候我们会为了一句诗、一个典故的解读在微信中一直探讨到凌晨……凡事最怕认真，如果认真还融入了热爱，那一定会触摸到一种深美闳约的境界。《四明雅韵》就是这样将对学术的认真与对传统文化的热爱兼容在一起的，我知道，那是辛红娟教授一直以来的坚持。

《四明雅韵——宁波古代诗歌英译》精心挑选的由唐及清关涉宁波的 60 首古典诗歌，分为"地理山水""禅道文化""风土佳物"与"酬赠送别"四大类，较为全面地覆盖到了千年宁波历史中的自然及人文风貌，呈现了诗意宁波的千姿百态。我自己长期从事中国古典诗词的研究与传播，且有着外语的求学背景，因而深知诗歌翻译的困境，尤其是中国古典诗歌的音律、意象（象征）、用典等诸多独有的特质，确乎很难信、达、雅地翻译成外语。然而，当我捧读这本《四明雅韵》的时候，我不得不佩服执笔译者张智中教授对于原诗的准确理解与翻译技巧的纯熟和巧妙。举个例子：我较为熟悉的唐代诗人许浑《晓发鄞江北渡寄崔韩二先辈》诗中有这样一句"露晓蒹葭重"，译者将之翻译为：

The morning reed is reedy in dew and dewdrops.

译者独具匠心地选择了 reed 和 reedy 两个单词分别表达"芦苇"以及"芦苇丛生的"意思，我尤其对用 reedy 来译"蒹葭重"赞叹不已。原诗显然是化用了《诗经》中"蒹葭苍苍，白露为霜"的意象，用一望无际的芦苇丛来表达一种视线的苍茫感，用联绵词"苍苍"增强音韵的美感。而译诗则以名词 reed 和形容词 reedy 组合，既运用英文诗歌的头韵法营造了类似于汉语联绵词的音韵与节奏美感，又呈现出了苍茫无际的芦苇丛的画面感，以此来凸显远行人内心的萧瑟与孤独情绪。dew 和 dewdrops 两个词的组合也有类似的妙用：除了以头韵强化联绵回环的韵律美，还以 dewdrops 将画面由静态转化为动态，在诗意的视觉呈现中又融入了时间的流动性，让人在反复吟咏之余真忍不住拍案叫绝！

类似于这样准确而又巧妙的安排，实在是体现了译者兼通两种语言及其文化内蕴的深厚功底。我深信，《四明雅韵——宁波古代诗歌英译》将引领着不同文化背景、不同语言背景的读者，一起走进绵延千年的宁波的诗情画意，领略萦绕在宁波的山山水水之间的古音雅韵，感受诗歌历史长河中宁波独具风情的自然之美与人文之美。

宁波并非"地穷山尽处"，而是中国悠长诗意中的一个重要驿站，当你在"诗意明州"里凝眸小驻，她一定会回馈给你别样的温柔与惊喜。

中央电视台《百家讲坛》栏目资深主讲人

《中国诗词大会》点评专家

杨 雨

2022 年 3 月 17 日

In the summer of 742, during the reign of emperor Tang Xuanzong, Li Bai, at his age of 42, bid farewell to Donglu (nowadays in Shandong Province), came with his family to Kuaiji (nowadays Shaoxing, Zhejiang Province) for sight-seeing, and he stayed with his Taoist-friend Wu Yun in Shanzhong (nowadays Shengzhou, Zhejiang Province). Thereafter, he toured around quite many legendary happy lands in Tiantai Range (Heavenly Terrace Range) and Siming Mountain (Mount Siming / All-Luminosity Mountain). Siming Mountain, a branch of Tiantai Range, spreads northeastward for one hundred and thirty *li*, with two hundred and eighty peaks towering into the sky, covering an area of over eight hundred square *li*. It boasts the highest peak with four caves which, in case of a high sky overflowing with pure air, look from afar like four transparent windows, and also look like four limpid eyes, through which the light of the sun and the moon and the stars penetrates, hence comes the name of "Four Windows" or Siming (Four Eyes All-Luminosity). Legend has it that, after crossing the sea, ancient immortals choose this mountain for their landing and take it as the nineth of the thirty-six heavenly abodes under the name of "the sky of crimson mountain and water".

Such a miraculous landscape and so mysterious a legend adorably captivate Li Bai, who "makes light of travelling to the distant Five Sacred Mountains in search of immortals and has an ardent love for scaling the well-known mountains".

Siming Mountain does not fail Li Bai in his expectation. In the poetry of Li Bai, Siming Mountain extends for "three thousand *li*": before sunrise the red glow spreads boundlessly and, at sunrise, the red glow is sprinkled into something like beautiful silk, surging and rolling glitteringly on steep snowy cliffs. Caught between the boundless sky and sea, Li Bai was beside himself with excitement, and he raised his arms heavenward, to heartily embrace the wagon of Azure Dragon, and the wagon of white tigers running toward him from the brilliant sunshine, which were actually the immortal officers to greet him. This gave him the feeling that he was driving a wagon together with the immortals through the clouds in the boundless ethereal air, whence he cast a glance down into the mortal world.

This very glamorous glance of Li Bai at Siming Mountain is regarded as the initiation of Ningbo into classical Chinese poetry: "The Siming Mountain, or All-Luminosity Mountain, extends for three thousand *li*, an early riser sees a town, crimson from the rosy clouds of dawn. Sunrise gives rise to a red glow: extending, spreading, sprinkling, until some beams shine brilliantly on steep snowy cliffs. Conducive to and healthful for a set of bowels — breathing rays of sunshine and imbibing jade-like liquid to produce cinnabar. Why are the hands raised so high? Suggestive of immortals riding Azure Dragon and White Tiger: I am ready to follow you to paradise." (*A Morning View of Sea-side Clouds* by Li Bai) And as it is magically fated: soon after Li Bai toured to the peak of Siming Mountain, his wagon of Azure Dragon and White Tiger really are running toward him — in the autumn of the same year, Li Bai, upon imperial order, lost no time hurrying to the capital of Chang'an (now Xi'an in Shaanxi Province), and "he starts off laughing heavenward", to embrace the "golden time" in his life to serve in the Imperial Academy. From then on, famous poet Li Bai's romantic literary pieces concerning Siming Mountain added luster to the legend of immotals here.

Ningbo got its ancient name of Siming after the majestic Siming Mountain in its realm, and its other name of Mingzhou also traces back to this very lofty multipeaked mountain. For Li Bai, the history of Mingzhou was not that long: Mingzhou was established in Maoxian County of Yuezhou in 738, while 4 years later it was re-administrated to be named as Yuyao Prefecture. And in 758, the city was named back into Mingzhou, which lasted until as late as in 1381 when it enjoyed its new and present name of Ningbo.

In classical Chinese poetry, Siming Mountain is the landmark of Mingzhou, which boasts mountains and seas, both immortal and Buddhistic. With majestic and beautiful landscapes the travellers' eyes can be feasted; with a long history and rich culture the literary men can delve into it; with its unique local conditions and customs the visitors can loiter and linger to stay. From generation to generation people who are born here or have ever lived here never stop telling their stories through writing — all these have contributed to the making of a poetic portrait of Mingzhou, and a cultural, historic Ningbo, a city which combines beauty and talent, emotion and wisdom.

In this respect, Ningbo shall be grateful to Li Bai and other ancient poets who have composed their poems and stories here, and thankful to the compilers and translators of *Poems Portraying Centuries-old City of Ningbo*: Professor Xin Hongjuan and Professor Zhang Zhizhong. Professor Xin Hongjuan is not a native of Ningbo, yet the rich cultural resources of Ningbo lend her inspiration in the making of this book. My acquaintance with Xin has been as long as 20 odd years, a host of years of having worked together in Central South University and, in spite of our different academic fields, there is, between us, a close connection and communication which, after she was transferred to Ningbo University, has been enhanced instead of decreased. Familiarity breeds knowledge: she has immersed herself in the field of translation for decades of years as a scholar who boasts a comprehensive and thorough understanding of traditional Chinese culture. And I heartily respect her for her diligence and conscientiousness. In the process of compiling and translating this bilingual verse collection with illustrations of woodblock style, she keeps talking about the poems with me through WeChat or mobile phone. Whenever I am on a business trip to Ningbo, she would, together with her team members, come to talk with me and, sometimes we would talk through WeChat until the wee hours simply for the meaning of a single line or the interpretation of a literary allusion. Nothing fails when earnestness is applied, particularly with passion, and a poetic realm of great beauty can be felt. The book is a combination of academic rigor and love for traditional culture, which, I believe, is the long-cherished pursuit of professor Xin.

Totaling 60 carefully selected Ningbo-related ancient Chinese poems from the Tang Dynasty to the Qing Dynasty, the four parts of *Poems Portraying Centuries-old City of Ningbo* : "Hills & Rills", "Zenism & Daoism", "Climate & Produce", and "Parting & Gift-presenting" well manifest the nature and humanity, as well as the charms and attractions of poetic Ningbo. For decades of years I am engaged in the study and interpretation of classical Chinese poems, coupled with my undergraduate major of French, I know very well the difficulties in poetry translation, particularly for classical Chinese poems, which possess unique qualities such as rhymes, images (symbols), and literary allusions — all contribute to the impossibility for them to be rendered faithfully, fluently, and elegantly into foreign languages. Yet, when I lay my hands on *Poems Portraying Centuries-old City of Ningbo*, I cannot but admire professor Zhang Zhizhong as an adept translator, both for his correct understanding of the ancient Chinese poems and for his consummate translation techniques. For example: in a poem entitled *To Two Seniors at the Northern Ferry of Yinjiang River* by Xu Hun, a famous Tang poet with whom I am familiar, there is such a line " 露晓蒹葭重 ", and the English version goes thus:

"The morning reed is reedy in dew and dewdrops".

The originality or creativeness of the translator manifests itself in his choice of "reed" and "reedy" to correspond with the two Chinese characters " 蒹葭 "(reed) and its suggestive meaning of "reedy", for which I am struck with admiration. Evidently, the poet, in writing this Chinese poem, has drawn inspiration from "the reeds and rushes are deeply green, / and the white dew is turned into hoarfrost", which are lines from the earliest source of classical Chinese poetry *The Book of Songs*. The poet expresses a dim view of vastness and boundlessness by dint of a limitless stretch or expanse of reedy grass, and by adopting the repetitive characters of " 苍苍 ", the beauty in sound is enhanced. In the translated poem, the noun "reed" is paired up with the adjective "reedy", hence alliteration which is commonly used in English poetry, to recreate beauty in sound and rhythm of the original poetic line, while exhibiting the picture of a great expanse of reedy field, so as to bring out the sense of solitude in the inmost recesses of the wanderer's mind. And the twin words of "dew" and "dewdrops" are similarly wonderful: in addition to alliteration to enhance the beauty of rhythm, the word "dewdrops" transforms the static picture into a dynamic one. In the revisualization of poetry, the mobility of time is fused therein — so much so that the reader is reduced to wonderment while reading and rereading with a taste and aftertaste.

Such accurate and felicitous choice of words and expressions, I suppose, cannot dispense with the translator's erudite knowledge in the two languages and their cultures. It is my belief that *Poems Portraying Centuries-old City of Ningbo* is going to appeal to the readers with various cultural backgrounds to learn more about Ningbo, a poetic city with a long history of over one thousand years, to feel the ancient melodious notes which are still lingering over the hills and rills of Ningbo, and to enjoy the unique beauty in nature and humanity of Ningbo through the long river of history.

Ningbo, though a city located "at the edge of land and mountain", has always been an important hub in the endlessly long line of Chinese poetry. When you come to stay to relax yourself in *Poems Portraying Centuries-old City of Ningbo*, you will be handsomely rewarded with a kind of particular warmth and pleasant surprise.

Yang Yu
Senior lecturer of the "Lecture Room" of CCTV
Comment expert of "The Chinese Poetry Competition" of CCTV
March 17, 2022

四明乃东南奥区，山川清淑，水木明瑟，繁景千汇，殊形万状，故称山水窟；襟山带海，蒸蔚云霞，洞天福地，氤氲仙道，故称灵仙窟宅；众流东委，西来释教，水涌金沙，地遍禅林，故称东南佛国；物产丰饶，地负海涵，曰珍曰错，富国养民，故称东南乐土；耕读不辍，弦歌相继，著书藏书，盈车充栋，室曰书窟，阁比琅嬛，故称文献之邦；运河入海，"江中船出海中去，洋外帆从天外来"，演为巨港；风物可人，"天然景物谁能状，千古诗人咏不休"，乃成诗窟。

四明"诗窟"之名，殊非浪得。灵境诗心，两相凑泊，物我交感，兴会空前。自唐迄今，诗人徜徉于此，诗思泉涌，诗作频生。总其历代诗歌数量之巨以万计，不禁令人击节，而发伙颐之叹！考其题材内容之丰富，举凡自然风光、人文景观、社会风俗、宗教文化、地方物产……无所不包。如此诗歌，乃四明之文化遗产，为世人了解、研究四明之珍贵文献；且又可资今世于此诗意栖居者，以及中外远来之游众，敲拍吟哦，助益其风物体认、审美鉴赏、人生情怀、精神境界，涵泳默化矣。

量大则需选本。历来选诗家，皆据选编之目的，确定选诗之原则与标准。时至今日，四明诗歌出现过较多选本，各具特色。今有宁波大学外国语学院博士生导师辛红娟教授、南开大学外国语学院博士生导师张智中教授，致力于传播中国传统文化，对四明之诗歌情有所钟，于"经典浙江"国际传播创新平台推出《四明雅韵——宁波古代诗歌英译》，精选四明诗歌经典，加以英文翻译。二位教授含菁咀华，采撷六十首诗歌，按照其题材内容，分作地理山水、禅道文化、风土佳物、酬赠送别四篇编译。所选作品颇具代表性，堪称四明诗歌之佳作。而将其译作英文，则又为传播四明诗歌、使其走向世界之创举。汉语古体诗歌，本为最难翻译之一种文体，难在意象意蕴、典故、作品内涵、意境等诸方面切实做到信、达、雅。二位教授自是精通中英双语翻译之专家，原本在中国典籍、汉语古诗之英译方面造诣深厚，成果出众，今乃举重若轻；每首诗歌，均以英语散体文、诗体、自由体三种体式译出，十分有趣，且读者可以据三种文体互为参照，领悟原作。四明诗歌得其传播世界，其功不可没，实可贺可赞也。

　　幸蒙嘱序，然言不尽意，谨道其崖略。

宁波大学人文与传媒学院教授

浙江省诗词楹联学会副会长

李亮伟

壬寅年桃月于甬上释然居

Siming (ancient elegant name of the now Ningbo) is a place in the southeast of China, with fair hills and limpid rills, where trees grow lushly to create a cluster of scenic spots with variegated shapes and scapes of the land, hence the name of "the cave of hills and rills with heavenly beauty". There is convergence of the mountain and the sea, where splendidly rosy clouds are wafting leisurely and spreading freely; as a heavenly abode overflowing with immortal air, it is known as "the immortal cave"; Buddhism was transmitted here from India, numerous Buddhist temples hither and thither, earned Siming name of "the land of Buddhism in southeast China". Having been a great producer and the ocean a great container of delicacies and dainties — a rich land with considerate caring for the people, it is also acknowledged as "the promised land". The sound of music and singing never ends while schooling goes on without interruption from generation to generation, books written and collected fill rooms after rooms, such a tremendous book collection is no smaller than that of the immortals, and it is thereby recognized as "the land of literature". It is the place where the canal runs into the sea, and the poetic line "along the river ships go ocean-bound; sails in the ocean come from beyond the horizon" portraits its being a busy port; "this scene of natural beauty defies description, in spite of poems composed by poets from generation to generation", this being the charm of the landscape, so to give the city name of "the cradle of poetry".

Siming as "the cradle of poetry" is not in vain. A poetic heart in a land of poetry, inspired mutually to produce poems of unparalleled beauty. From the Tang Dynasty downward to now, countless poets linger here with a ready source of inspiration, so as to have guaranteed a great wealth of poems. Spanning all ages, the poems totalling up to over ten thousand pieces have drawn admiration and acclaimation. There is a whole gamut of themes or subject matters, ranging from natural scenery to human landscape, to social customs, to religious culture, and to local produce… thoroughly comprehensive. Such poems are the cultural heritage of Ningbo, as rare and treasured literature for people to get to know and study Ningbo; and they can enrich the poetic mind of the dwellers here, while providing entertainment for visitors from places both domestic and foreign. These poems can, physically and spiritually, lead us to the names of local things and subject our mind under aesthetic experience so as to enrich our feelings and broaden our mental realm, without our awareness.

Such a great number of poems calls for a selection, and the compilers through various ages do this in accordance with their different purposes, principles, and standards. Up to now, there have been a host of selections from the poems about Ningbo, each with their unique features. Now Xin Hongjuan, professor and doctoral supervisor of the Faculty of Foreign Languages of Ningbo University, joins hands with Zhang Zhizhong, professor and doctoral supervisor of the College of Foreign Languages of Nankai University, to dissipate traditional Chinese culture, while cherishing a deep love for the poetry of Ningbo, and through the innovation platform of "Zhejiang Classics Going Global" they produce *Poems Portraying Centuries-old City of Ningbo* with a fabulous selection of Ningbo poetry, coupled with English translation. The two professors choose 60 Ningbo-related poems which are, in accordance with their contents, categorized into four parts: "Hills & Rills", "Zenism & Daoism", "Climate & Produce", and "Parting & Gift-presenting". Quite representative, the poetic pieces are equal to the excellent poems of Ningbo. With correspondent English versions, they undertake a pioneering work of dissipating Ningbo poetry and making it global. Classical Chinese poems, as a literary genre, defy translation, with challenges and difficulties in reproducing the original images, meaning, connotation, and poetic realm, etc. — faithfully, fluently, and elegantly. Yet the two professors, as experts in the translation field, are well established in the English translation of Chinese classics and ancient Chinese poems with their outstanding achievements, so they undertake the task without too many strained efforts. The English translation of each poem has three styles: prose style, poetic style, and free style, which is of great significance for the readers to approach the original Chinese poems. The globalization of Ningbo poetry cannot dispense with their contribution, and their meritorious deeds cannot be obliterated, and I would like to take this opportunity to offer my warmest congratulations.

The preface is written upon request, yet my words fail to convey what I have in my mind, hence a rough sketch of it.

Li Liangwei

Professor of the School of Journalism and Communication of Ningbo University

Vice-chairman of Zhejiang Provincial Association of Chinese Poetry & Couplets

March, 2022

Study of Relief, Ningbo

地理山水
Hills & Rills

禅道文化
Zenism & Daoism

风土佳物
Climate & Produce

酬赠送别
Parting & Gift-presenting

地理山水

Hills & Rills

早望海霞边

A Morning View of Sea-side Clouds

早望海霞边

［唐］李　白

四明三千里，朝起赤城霞。

日出红光散，分辉照雪崖。

一餐咽琼液，五内发金沙。

举手何所待，青龙白虎车。

A Morning View of Sea-side Clouds

[Tang Dynasty] Li Bai

散体译文：

The Siming Mountain, or All-Luminosity Mountain, extends for three thousand miles, an early riser sees a town, crimson from the rosy clouds of dawn. Sunrise gives rise to a red glow: extending, spreading, sprinkling, until some beams shine brilliantly on steep snowy cliffs. Conducive to and healthful for a set of bowels — breathing rays of sunshine and imbibing jade-like liquid to produce cinnabar. Why are the hands raised so high? Suggestive of immortals riding Azure Dragon and White Tiger: I am ready to follow you to paradise.

诗体译文：

The Siming Mountain, or All-Luminosity Mountain extends for three thousand miles, an early riser sees a town, crimson from the rosy clouds of dawn. Sunrise gives rise to a red glow: extending, spreading, sprinkling, until some beams shine brilliantly on steep snowy cliffs. Conducive to and healthful for a set of bowels — breathing

rays of sunshine and imbibing jade-like liquid to produce cinnabar.
Why are the hands raised so high? Suggestive of immortals riding
Azure Dragon and White Tiger: I am ready to follow you to paradise.

自由体译文：

The Siming Mountain, or All-Luminosity Mountain

extends for three thousand miles, an early riser

sees a town, crimson from the rosy clouds of dawn.

Sunrise gives rise to a red glow:

extending, spreading, sprinkling,

until some beams shine brilliantly

on steep snowy cliffs.

Conducive to and healthful for

a set of bowels — breathing rays

of sunshine and imbibing jade-like liquid

to produce cinnabar. Why are the hands

raised so high? Suggestive of immortals

riding Azure Dragon and White Tiger:

I am ready to follow you

to paradise.

Translator's note:

① Siming Mountain, literal translation is All-Luminosity or All-Luminosity Mountain, extending between Ningbo and Shaoxing in Zhejiang Province, hereinafter referred to as All-Luminosity Mountain.

② Azure Dragon (Cyan Dragon), White Tiger, together with Black Tortoise and Vermilion Bird are believed to be China's four great beasts.

游四窗

Touring the All-Luminosity Mountain

游四窗

[唐] 刘长卿

四明山绝奇，自古说登陆。
苍崖倚天立，覆石如覆屋。
玲珑开户牖，落落明四目。
箕星分南野，有斗挂檐北。
日月居东西，朝昏互出没。
我来游其间，寄傲巾半幅。
白云本无心，悠然伴幽独。
对此脱尘鞅，顿忘荣与辱。
长笑天地宽，仙风吹佩玉。

Touring the All-Luminosity Mountain

[Tang Dynasty] Liu Zhangqing

散体译文：

　　Unsurpassably wonderful is the All-Luminosity Mountain, a landward sight spot since time of yore. The steep cliff points heavenward, forming a canopy of rocks, as if to cover a house. The peak of peaks boasts four window-shaped caves, fair like four bright eyes in the sky. Winnow Basket, one of the twenty-eight lunar mansions, hangs in the southern sky when the Big Dipper hangs north of the eaves. The sun and the moon move eastward or westward, and alternately appear or disappear. As a visitor I come, I see, leisurely, restfully, slovenly. The white clouds, mindless, careless, wafting and drifting slowly, sluggishly, seclusively. The sight deprives people of social shackles and conventional manacles; honor and disgrace vanish into the highest heavens. With long laughter, heaven and earth are boundless; jade pendants gently blown in the immortal wind.

诗体译文:

Unsurpassably wonderful is the All-Luminosity
Mountain, a landward sight spot since time of
yore. The steep cliff points heavenward, forming
a canopy of rocks, as if to cover a house. The peak
of peaks boasts four window-shaped caves, fair
like four bright eyes in the sky. Winnow Basket, one of the
twenty-eight lunar mansions, hangs in the southern
sky when the Big Dipper hangs north of the eaves.
The sun and the moon move eastward or westward,
and alternately appear or disappear. As a visitor
I come, I see, leisurely, restfully, slovenly.
The white clouds, mindless, careless, wafting
and drifting slowly, sluggishly, seclusively.
The sight deprives people of social shackles
and conventional manacles; honor and disgrace
vanish into the highest heavens. With long
laughter, heaven and earth are boundless; jade
pendants gently blown in the immortal wind.

自由体译文:

Unsurpassably wonderful is the All-Luminosity Mountain,
a landward sight spot since time of yore. The steep cliff
points heavenward, forming a canopy of rocks,
as if to cover a house. The peak of peaks boasts four window-shaped

caves, fair like four bright eyes in the sky. Winnow Basket, one of
the twenty-eight lunar mansions, hangs in the southern sky
when the Big Dipper hangs north of the eaves.
The sun and the moon move eastward or westward,
and alternately appear or disappear.
As a visitor I come, I see,
leisurely, restfully, slovenly.
The white clouds, mindless, careless, wafting and drifting
slowly, sluggishly, seclusively.
The sight deprives people of social shackles
and conventional manacles; honor
and disgrace vanish into the highest heavens.
With long laughter, heaven and earth
are boundless; jade pendants gently blown
in the immortal wind.

同诸隐者夜登四明山

［唐］施肩吾

半夜寻幽上四明，手攀松桂触云行。
相呼已到无人境，何处玉箫吹一声？

同诸隐者夜登四明山
Climbing the All-Luminosity Mountain at Night with Hermits

Climbing the All-Luminosity Mountain at Night with Hermits

[Tang Dynasty] Shi Jianwu

散体译文：

Seeking seclusion in midnight, we climb the All-Luminosity Mountain; hands touching pines and trees of cherry bay, heads scraping the clouds. Progressively, we seem to come to a realm without a single soul. A flute is traveling: from where?

诗体译文：

Seeking seclusion in midnight, we climb the All-Luminosity
Mountain; hands touching pines and trees of cherry bay,
heads scraping the clouds. Progressively, we seem to come to
a realm without a single soul. A flute is traveling: from where?

自由体译文：

Seeking seclusion in midnight, we
climb the All-Luminosity Mountain;
hands touching pines and trees of cherry bay,
heads scraping the clouds.
Progressively, we seem to come
to a realm without a single soul.
A flute is traveling:
from where?

宿四明山

［唐］施肩吾

黎洲老人命余宿，杳然高顶浮云平。
下视不知几千仞，欲晓不晓天鸡声。

宿四明山

Lodging in the All-Luminosity Mountain

Lodging in the All-Luminosity Mountain

[Tang Dynasty] Shi Jianwu

散体译文：

The old mountaineer detains me for lodging overnight; his heavenly roof towers into the wafting white clouds. Looking down unfathomably for thousands of miles; whether at or before the break of day, a celestial rooster crows.

诗体译文：

The old mountaineer detains me for lodging overnight;

his heavenly roof towers into the wafting white clouds.

Looking down unfathomably for thousands of miles;

whether at or before the break of day, a celestial rooster crows.

自由体译文：

The old mountaineer detains me

for lodging overnight; his heavenly

roof towers into the wafting white clouds.

Looking down unfathomably

for thousands of miles;

whether at or before the break of day,

a celestial rooster

crows.

忆四明山泉

［唐］施肩吾

爱彼山中石泉水，幽声夜落虚窗里。
至今忆得卧云时，犹自涓涓在人耳。

忆四明山泉

Remembering the Mountain Spring of All-Luminosity Mountain

Remembering the Mountain Spring of All-Luminosity Mountain

[Tang Dynasty] Shi Jianwu

散体译文：

Loveable is the rocky spring. Water, babbling and gurgling, falls from night to night into profound emptiness of seclusion. I still remember those lazy, leisurely days of lying in clouds — the sound of slow and sluggish trickling lingers in the ears.

诗体译文：

Loveable is the rocky spring. Water, babbling and gurgling,

falls from night to night into profound emptiness of seclusion.

I still remember those lazy, leisurely days of lying in clouds —

the sound of slow and sluggish trickling lingers in the ears.

自由体译文：

Loveable is the rocky spring.

Water, babbling and gurgling, falls from night

to night into profound emptiness

of seclusion. I still remember those

lazy, leisurely days of lying in clouds —

the sound of slow and sluggish

trickling lingers

in the ears.

游雪窦寺

〔唐〕方　干

绝顶空王宅，香风满薜萝。
地高春色晚，天近日光多。
流水随寒玉，遥峰拥翠波。
前山有丹凤，云外一声过。

游雪窦寺
Touring Xuedou Temple

Touring Xuedou Temple

[Tang Dynasty] Fang Gan

散体译文：

The mountain tiptop embraces a Buddhist temple, which is choked with free growers fragrant in spring wind. Its great height delays spring, which lingers and lengthens; the sky approachable, more brilliance of sunshine. Creek water meanders like clear and cold jade; distant peaks embrace green peaks upon green peaks like green waves. There are phoenixes in the opposite mountain; a single cry, traveling from beyond clouds, falls pleasantly on the ear.

诗体译文：

The mountain tiptop embraces a Buddhist temple, which
is choked with free growers fragrant in spring wind. Its
great height delays spring, which lingers and lengthens;
the sky approachable, more brilliance of sunshine. Creek
water meanders like clear and cold jade; distant peaks
embrace green peaks upon green peaks like green waves. There
are phoenixes in the opposite mountain; a single cry,
traveling from beyond clouds, falls pleasantly on the ear.

自由体译文：

The mountain tiptop embraces
a Buddhist temple, which is choked
with free growers fragrant
in spring wind. Its great height
delays spring, which lingers
and lengthens; the sky approachable,

more brilliance of sunshine.

Creek water meanders

like clear and cold jade;

distant peaks embrace green peaks

upon green peaks like green waves.

There are phoenixes in the opposite mountain;

a single cry, traveling from beyond clouds,

falls pleasantly

on the ear.

Translator's note:

Xuedou Temple, a major scenic spot in Xuedou Mountain (also known as Snow-Capped Mountain), was originally founded in the Tang Dynasty. "Xuedou" literally means snow-capped.

题龙泉寺绝顶

Inscription on the Lofty Dragon Spring Temple

题龙泉寺绝顶

［唐］方　干

未明先见海底日，良久远鸡方报晨。
古树含风常带雨，寒岩四月始知春。
中天气爽星河近，下界时丰雷雨均。
前后登临思无尽，年年改换往来人。

Inscription on the Lofty Dragon Spring Temple

[Tang Dynasty] Fang Gan

散体译文：

　　Before daybreak, from lofty height of the temple, a sun is rising from the depths of the sea; after a great while, a rooster crows to welcome a new morning. Ancient trees are billowing and bellowing with raindrops in the wind; cool and cold rocks know no spring until May. In mid-air clear and crisp, the river of stars is within reach; in the world of worldlings, there is a good crop out of a good timely rain. Once more to the lofty heights of Dragon Spring Temple — imagination runs wild; from year to year visitors change, but the temple stands — and stays.

诗体译文：

　　Before daybreak, from lofty height of the temple, a sun is rising from
the depths of the sea; after a great while, a rooster crows to welcome
a new morning. Ancient trees are billowing and bellowing with
raindrops in the wind; cool and cold rocks know no spring until May.
In mid-air clear and crisp, the river of stars is within reach; in the world

of worldlings, there is a good crop out of a good timely rain. Once more to the lofty heights of Dragon Spring Temple — imagination runs wild; from year to year visitors change, but the temple stands — and stays.

自由体译文：

Before daybreak, from lofty height

of the temple, a sun is rising

from the depths of the sea;

after a great while, a rooster crows

to welcome a new morning.

Ancient trees are billowing and bellowing

with raindrops in the wind;

cool and cold rocks know no spring

until May. In mid-air

clear and crisp, the river of stars

is within reach; in the world of worldlings,

there is a good crop out of a good timely rain.

Once more to the lofty heights

of Dragon Spring Temple — imagination

runs wild; from year to year

visitors change, but the temple

stands — and

stays.

归四明

Journey Back to the All-Luminosity Mountain

归四明

［宋］胡幽贞

海色连四明，仙舟去容易。
天籍岂辄问，不是卑朝士。

Journey Back to the All-Luminosity Mountain

[Song Dynasty] Hu Youzhen

散体译文：

The color of the sea merges with the Mountain of All-Luminosity, when the celestial boat easily speeds away. If you ask about my native place in heaven — not an official in the imperial court.

诗体译文：

The color of the sea merges with the Mountain
of All-Luminosity, when the celestial boat easily
speeds away. If you ask about my native place
in heaven — not an official in the imperial court.

自由体译文：

The color of the sea merges
with the Mountain of All-Luminosity
when the celestial boat easily speeds away.
If you ask about my native
place in heaven —
not an official
in the imperial court.

姜山五峰咏·金鸡峰

[五代] 释延寿

松萝高镇夏长寒，透出群峰画恐难。
造化功成彰五德，洞天云散露花冠。

姜山五峰咏·金鸡峰
Ode to Five Peaks of Jiangshan Mountain: To Golden Rooster Peak

Ode to Five Peaks of Jiangshan Mountain: To Golden Rooster Peak

[The Five Dynasties] Shi Yanshou

散体译文：

Pines and vines twist, tangle, enlace, entwine, bringing coolness in height of summer; the foliage reveals dim and distant peaks, defying delineation. With creative powers the Creator has created the Golden Rooster Peak, symbolic of five virtues; daybreak clouds dispersing, a flowery crest exhibits itself.

诗体译文：

Pines and vines twist, tangle, enlace, entwine, bringing coolness in height
of summer; the foliage reveals dim and distant peaks, defying delineation.
With creative powers the Creator has created the Golden Rooster Peak,
symbolic
of five virtues; daybreak clouds dispersing, a flowery crest exhibits itself.

自由体译文：

Pines and vines twist, tangle, enlace, entwine,
bringing coolness in height of summer;
the foliage reveals dim and distant peaks,
defying delineation. With creative powers
the Creator has created the Golden Rooster Peak,
symbolic of five virtues; daybreak
clouds dispersing, a flowery crest
exhibits itself.

姜山五峰咏·蛾眉峰

［五代］释延寿

盘空势险露岩根，深洞声寒落石泉。

好是雨余江上见，水云僧出认西天。

姜山五峰咏·蛾眉峰
Ode to Five Peaks of Jiangshan Mountain: To Eyebrows Peak

Ode to Five Peaks of Jiangshan Mountain: To Eyebrows Peak

[The Five Dynasties] Shi Yanshou

散体译文：

Circling, whirling in the air, steep and precipitous — rocky roots are exposed; caves deep, sounds chilly — stony springs cascade. A fair view of Eyebrows Peak from the river washed by rain; a wandering monk knows his location by pointing to the sky in the west.

诗体译文：

Circling, whirling in the air, steep and precipitous — rocky roots are exposed; caves deep, sounds chilly —stony springs cascade.

A fair view of Eyebrows Peak from the river washed by rain;

a wandering monk knows his location by pointing to the sky in the west.

自由体译文：

Circling, whirling in the air,

steep and precipitous — rocky roots

are exposed; caves deep, sounds chilly —

stony springs cascade.

A fair view of Eyebrows Peak

from the river washed by rain;

a wandering monk knows his location

by pointing to the sky

in the west.

姜山五峰咏·积翠峰

［五代］释延寿

翠压群峰地形直，落日猿声在空碧。
天风吹散断崖云，古松长露三秋色。

姜山五峰咏·积翠峰
Ode to Five Peaks of Jiangshan Mountain: To Green-Amassing Peak

Ode to Five Peaks of Jiangshan Mountain: To Green-Amassing Peak

[The Five Dynasties] Shi Yanshou

散体译文：

The green of Green-Amassing Peak overshadows all the other green tops; against the setting sun travels the green cry of apes from a green depth of woods in the green air. The heavenly wind scatters the clouds over broken cliffs; age-old pine trees tinted with unfading autumnal green.

诗体译文：

The green of Green-Amassing Peak overshadows all the other green

tops; against the setting sun travels the green cry of apes from a green

depth of woods in the green air. The heavenly wind scatters the clouds

over broken cliffs; age-old pine trees tinted with unfading autumnal

green.

自由体译文：

The green of Green-Amassing Peak overshadows
all the other green tops; against the setting sun
travels the green cry of apes from a green depth
of woods in the green air.
The heavenly wind scatters the clouds
over broken cliffs; age-old pine trees
tinted with unfading
autumnal green.

姜山五峰咏·凌云峰

［五代］释延寿

烟萝高巇势凌云，影泻斜阳出海门。
曾与支公探隐去，夜寒雷雨上方闻。

姜山五峰咏·凌云峰
Ode to Five Peaks of Jiangshan Mountain: To Cloud-Kissing Peak

Ode to Five Peaks of Jiangshan Mountain: To Cloud-Kissing Peak

[The Five Dynasties] Shi Yanshou

散体译文:

Misty vines covering heights over heights, skyward and clouds-kissing; the slanting sun vomits a river-like shadow meandering eastward out of sea-gate. In search of a seclusive place in the depths of the mountain with a bosom friend; the chilly night is lending an ear to a thunderstorm in the sky of skies.

诗体译文:

Misty vines covering heights over heights, skyward and clouds-kissing; the slanting sun vomits a river-like shadow meandering eastward out of sea-gate. In search of a seclusive place in the depths of the mountain with a bosom friend; the chilly night is lending an ear to a thunderstorm in the sky of skies.

自由体译文:

Misty vines covering heights over heights,

skyward and clouds-kissing;

the slanting sun vomits a river-like shadow

meandering eastward out of sea-gate.

In search of a seclusive place

in the depths of the mountain

with a bosom friend; the chilly night

is lending an ear to a thunderstorm

in the sky of skies.

姜山五峰咏·白马峰

[五代] 释延寿

湖外层峰泻危瀑，天际阴阴长寒木。
南北行人望莫穷，秋云一片横幽谷。

姜山五峰咏·白马峰
Ode to Five Peaks of Jiangshan Mountain: To White Horse Peak

Ode to Five Peaks of Jiangshan Mountain: To White Horse Peak

[The Five Dynasties] Shi Yanshou

散体译文：

Beyond the lake, peaks upon peaks are noisy with precipitous waterfalls. The horizon of horizons is dim and murky with lush trees coolly green. Travellers to and fro are streaming like a constantly running creek, while a stretch of white clouds waft and float over secluded valleys.

诗体译文：

Beyond the lake, peaks upon peaks are noisy with precipitous water-falls. The horizon of horizons is dim and murky with lush trees coolly green. Travellers to and fro are streaming like a constantly running creek, while a stretch of white clouds waft and float over secluded valleys.

自由体译文：

Beyond the lake, peaks upon peaks
are noisy with precipitous waterfalls.
The horizon of horizons
is dim and murky
with lush trees coolly green.
Travellers to and fro
are streaming like a constantly
running creek, while a stretch
of white clouds waft
and float over
secluded valleys.

候涛山
Houtao Mountain

候涛山

[宋] 应 傃

闾尾苍茫四际同，嵬峨岩石奠城东。
云连波白蒸鳌柱，月带潮青结蜃宫。
夹树烟笼花气舞，半炉香映日光融。
苍藤满砌依岚翠，应许乘槎贯斗中。

Houtao Mountain

[Song Dynasty] Ying You

散体译文：

　　Rocky and lofty is the mountain, towering to the east of the town, whose lanes and streets are invariably dim and distant. Churning with white waves and coiling clouds, heavenward columns are bathed here and there; in moonlight tinged with green mist, hazy mirages are forming. Trees are misty with flying flowers as if dancing, and half-hidden furnaces fuse into the sunlight. Rattans and vines flourish into massy growth and undergrowth all over the mountain — a green sea where floating rafts can go heavenward to scrape the Great Dipper.

诗体译文：

　　Rocky and lofty is the mountain, towering to the east of the town,
　　whose lanes and streets are invariably dim and distant.
　　Churning with white waves and coiling clouds, heavenward
　　columns are bathed here and there; in moonlight tinged with green mist,

hazy mirages are forming. Trees are misty with flying flowers as if dancing,

and half-hidden furnaces fuse into the sunlight. Rattans and vines flourish

into massy growth and undergrowth all over the mountain —

a green sea where floating rafts can go heavenward to scrape the Great Dipper.

自由体译文：

Rocky and lofty is the mountain

towering to the east of the town,

whose lanes and streets

are invariably dim and distant.

Churning with white waves and coiling clouds,

heavenward columns are bathed here and there;

in moonlight tinged with green mist,

hazy mirages are forming.

Trees are misty with flying flowers as if dancing,

and half-hidden furnaces fuse into the sunlight.

Rattans and vines flourish into massy growth

and undergrowth all over the mountain —

a green sea where floating rafts

can go heavenward to scrape

the Great Dipper.

千丈岩瀑布

〔宋〕王安石

拔地万重清嶂立，悬空千丈素流分。
共看玉女机丝挂，映日还成五色文。

千丈岩瀑布
Qianzhang Rock Waterfall

Qianzhang Rock Waterfall

[Song Dynasty] Wang Anshi

散体译文：

Rising sheer from level ground, precipitous cliffs upon cliffs tower heavenward. The waterfall cascades down for thousands of feet where the white water divides — seemingly into white silk woven by the Celestial Girl, which is charmed into five colors by the slanting sunlight.

诗体译文：

Rising sheer from level ground, precipitous cliffs upon cliffs tower
heavenward. The waterfall cascades down for thousands of feet
where the white water divides — seemingly into white silk woven by
the Celestial Girl, which is charmed into five colors by the slanting
sunlight.

自由体译文：

Rising sheer from level ground,
precipitous cliffs upon cliffs tower
heavenward. The waterfall cascades down
for thousands of feet where
the white water divides —
seemingly into white silk woven by
the Celestial Girl, which is charmed
into five colors by the slanting sunlight.

Translator's note:

In front of Xuedou Temple, there is a waterfall called Xuedou Waterfall, also known as Qianzhang Rock Waterfall. Qianzhang literally means thousands of feet. The water head is in the valleys at the south and the north of Xuedou Temple. The water of the Milk Spring flows into Jinjing Pool, an ancient pool developed in the Southern Song Dynasty, crossing Guanshan Bridge and pouring out of the cliff mouth.

寒食过东钱湖

［元］袁士元

尽说西湖足胜游，东湖谁信更清幽。
一百五日客身过，七十二溪春水流。
白鸟影边霞屿寺，翠微深处月波楼。
天然景物谁能状，千古诗人咏不休。

寒食过东钱湖

Passing by Dongqian Lake on the Cold Food Festival

Passing by Dongqian Lake on the Cold Food Festival

[Yuan Dynasty] Yuan Shiyuan

散体译文:

It is universally acknowledged the West Lake is beauty itself as a scenic spot, but who believes Dongqian Lake is more limpid and tranquil? A hundred and five days after winter solstice it is the Cold Food Day; Dongqian Lake is constantly fed by seventy two spring streams. Side by side with the flitting shadows of aigrettes is the Xiayu Temple; stowed away in the depth of great masses of emerald mountain is the Yuebo Tower. This scene of natural beauty defies description, in spite of poems composed by poets from generation to generation.

诗体译文:

It is universally acknowledged the West Lake is beauty itself as a
scenic spot, but who believes Dongqian Lake is more limpid and
tranquil? A hundred and five days after winter solstice it is the Cold
Food Day; Dongqian Lake is constantly fed by seventy two spring
streams. Side by side with the flitting shadows of aigrettes is the Xiayu
Temple; stowed away in the depth of great masses of emerald mountain
is the Yuebo Tower. This scene of natural beauty defies description,
in spite of poems composed by poets from generation to generation.

自由体译文:

It is universally acknowledged the West Lake
is beauty itself as a scenic spot, but who believes
Dongqian Lake is more limpid and tranquil?
A hundred and five days after winter solstice

it is the Cold Food Day; Dongqian Lake is

constantly fed by seventy two spring streams.

Side by side with the flitting shadows

of aigrettes is the Xiayu Temple;

stowed away in the depth of great masses

of emerald mountain is the Yuebo Tower.

This scene of natural beauty defies description,

in spite of poems composed by poets

from generation to generation.

Translator's note:

The Cold Food Festival (Day) is a traditional Chinese holiday celebrated for three consecutive days starting from the day before the Qingming Festival around April 5 every year. It is celebrated in China as well as its neighboring regions such as Korea and Vietnam. In this time of year, the sky becomes clearer and buds sprout in the field. Farmers sow various seeds and supply water to their rice paddies. The traditionally practiced activities during the Cold Food Festival includes eating cold ready-made food, the visitation of ancestral tombs, cock-fighting, going-outing, playing on swings, beating out blankets (to freshen them), and tug-of-war, etc.

禅道文化

Zenism & Daoism

送萧炼师入四明山
To Taoist Xiao Bound for the All-Luminosity Mountain

送萧炼师入四明山

［唐］孟　郊

闲于独鹤心，大于高松年。
迥出万物表，高栖四明巅。
千寻直裂峰，百尺倒泻泉。
绛雪为我饭，白云为我田。
静言不语俗，灵踪时步天。

To Taoist Xiao Bound for the All-Luminosity Mountain

[Tang Dynasty] Meng Jiao

散体译文：

More idle and leisurely than a solitary crane, enjoying a greater age than that of a pine tree. The lofty peak towers over the mortal world, taking its perch on the top of the All-Luminosity Mountain. The cliff with a height of thousands of feet is made of irregular rough rocks, and the waterfall with a length of hundreds of feet falls plump into the abyss. The Taoist's snowy elixir is your food, and the stretch of white clouds is the field for you to grow medical plants. Few of words, you are never wordy about mortal things; you scale occasionally to some spot — to observe the way of heaven.

诗体译文：

More idle and leisurely than a solitary crane, enjoying a
greater age than that of a pine tree. The lofty peak towers
over the mortal world, taking its perch on the top of the All-

Luminosity Mountain. The cliff with a height of thousands of feet is made of irregular rough rocks, and the waterfall with a length of hundreds of feet falls plump into the abyss. The Taoist's snowy elixir is your food, and the stretch of white clouds is the field for you to grow medical plants. Few of words, you are never wordy about mortal things; you scale occasionally to some spot — to observe the way of heaven.

自由体译文：

More idle and leisurely than a solitary crane,
enjoying a greater age than that of a pine tree.
The lofty peak towers over the mortal world,
taking its perch on the top of the All-Luminosity
Mountain. The cliff with a height of thousands of feet
is made of irregular rough rocks, and the waterfall
with a length of hundreds of feet falls plump into the abyss.
The Taoist's snowy elixir is your food,
and the stretch of white clouds is the field
for you to grow medical plants.
Few of words, you are never wordy
about mortal things;
you scale occasionally
to some spot — to observe
the way of heaven.

四明兰若赠寂禅师
To a Buddhist Monk in the Depth of Woods

四明兰若赠寂禅师

〔唐〕周 贺

丛木开风径，过从白昼寒。
舍深原草合，茶疾竹薪干。
夕雨生眠兴，禅心少话端。
频来觉无事，尽日坐相看。

To a Buddhist Monk in the Depth of Woods

[Tang Dynasty] Zhou He

散体译文:

A windy path snakes through dense woods to a Buddhist temple; even when walking along it midday, coldness is felt. The room is choked with grassy green; dry bamboos as firewood to boil tea speedily. Evening rain breeds drowsiness; a Zen heart communicates without the aid of words. A frequenter has no business to get down to, except for daylong facing each other.

诗体译文:

A windy path snakes through dense woods
to a Buddhist temple; even when walking along it
midday, coldness is felt. The room is choked
with grassy green; dry bamboos as firewood
to boil tea speedily. Evening rain breeds drowsiness; a Zen heart communicates without the aid

of words. A frequenter has no business to get
down to, except for daylong facing each other.

自由体译文：

A windy path snakes through dense woods
to a Buddhist temple; even when
walking along it midday, coldness is felt.
The room is choked with grassy green;
dry bamboos as firewood
to boil tea speedily. Evening rain
breeds drowsiness; a Zen heart
communicates without the aid
of words. A frequenter
has no business to get down to,
except for daylong
facing each other.

範處士在育王寺書碑因以寄贈

Fan Di's Inscription on the Stone Tablet at Ashoka Temple

范处士在育王寺书碑因以寄赠

［唐］于季友

墨妙复辞雄，扁舟访远公。
云天书梵字，霜月步莲宫。
迹寄双林下，名留劫石中。
遥知松径望，栗叶满山红。

Fan Di's Inscription on the Stone Tablet at Ashoka Temple

[Tang Dynasty] Yu Jiyou

散体译文：

　　Both the calligraphy and writing of my friend Fan Di are unrivalled; a boat brings me to the temple in search of a distinguished monk. Sanskrit words are written in the sky heavy with clouds; the frosty moon is lingering in the lotus palace. Lodging in the temple of double forests, an inscription is made on the stone tablet, where a list of names are carved to last forever. Looking along the path lined with pines, the mountain is flamboyant with flickering chestnut trees.

诗体译文：

　　Both the calligraphy and writing of my friend Fan Di are
　　unrivalled; a boat brings me to the temple in search of a
　　distinguished monk. Sanskrit words are written in the sky
　　heavy with clouds; the frosty moon is lingering in the
　　lotus palace. Lodging in the temple of double forests, an
　　inscription is made on the stone tablet, where a list of names

are carved to last forever. Looking along the path lined
with pines, the mountain is flamboyant with flickering chestnut trees.

自由体译文：

Both the calligraphy and writing

of my friend Fan Di are unrivalled;

a boat brings me to the temple

in search of a distinguished monk.

Sanskrit words are written in the sky

heavy with clouds; the frosty moon

is lingering in the lotus palace.

Lodging in the temple of double forests,

an inscription is made on the stone tablet,

where a list of names are carved to last

forever. Looking along the path

lined with pines, the mountain

is flamboyant with flickering

chestnut trees.

时在育王寺书石字奉酬中丞使君寄赠四韵依次用本韵

In Reply to My Friend Yu Jiyou

时在育王寺书石字奉酬中丞使君寄赠四韵依次用本韵

〔唐〕范　的

拙艺荷才雄，新诗起谢公。

开缄光佛域，望景动星宫。

风雪文章里，书镌琬琰中。

将谁比佳句？霞绮散成红。

In Reply to My Friend Yu Jiyou

[Tang Dynasty] Fan Di

散体译文：

My awkward calligraphy is tempered by your vigorous writing; new-style poetry begins from the writing of Xie Tiao. When I open to read your poem sent to me, the temple is graced with light; bethinking myself of your form, it seems the star of literary talent is twinkling in the palace. Seasonal landscapes appear in your literary pieces, which are carved on the tablets. What poetic lines can be matched with your famous lines? Only "beautiful clouds scatter into red dots" by Xie Tiao.

诗体译文：

My awkward calligraphy is tempered by your vigorous
writing; new-style poetry begins from the writing of Xie Tiao.
When I open to read your poem sent to me, the temple is graced
with light; bethinking myself of your form, it seems the star
of literary talent is twinkling in the palace. Seasonal landscapes
appear in your literary pieces, which are carved on the tablets.

What poetic lines can be matched with your famous lines?

Only "beautiful clouds scatter into red dots" by Xie Tiao.

自由体译文：

My awkward calligraphy is tempered

by your vigorous writing;

new-style poetry begins from the writing

of Xie Tiao. When I open to read your poem

sent to me, the temple is graced with light;

bethinking myself of your form,

it seems the star of literary talent

is twinkling in the palace.

Seasonal landscapes appear

in your literary pieces,

which are carved on the tablets.

What poetic lines can be matched

with your famous lines? Only

"beautiful clouds scatter into red dots"

by Xie Tiao.

题四明金鹅寺壁

Inscription on the Wall of Golden Goose Temple

题四明金鹅寺壁

［唐］吕　岩

方丈有门出不钥，见个山童露双脚。

问伊方丈何寂寥，道是虚空也不著。

闻此语，何欣欣，主翁岂是寻常人。

我来谒见不得见，谒心耿耿生埃尘。

归去也，波浩渺，路入蓬莱山杳杳。

相思一上石楼时，雪晴海阔千峰晓。

Inscription on the Wall of Golden Goose Temple

[Tang Dynasty] Lü Yan

散体译文：

　　The abbot leaves the temple without locking the gate, and I find a mountain boy greeting me barefooted, whom I ask why the temple is so secluded and solitary? — Even if it is emptiness itself, we do not mind. At the boy's words I am immensely delighted, believing his master no common monk. Failure to meet the person himself fills my heart with admiration of a mortal being. Helpless, I return by the road leading to Mount Penglai, a boundless expanse of misty waves and rolling waters. Immersed in pining, I climb atop the tower, to see snowy peaks upon peaks brilliant against a boundless sea.

诗体译文：

　　The abbot leaves the temple without locking the gate,

and I find a mountain boy greeting me barefooted,

whom I ask why the temple is so secluded and solitary?

— Even if it is emptiness itself, we do not mind. At

the boy's words I am immensely delighted, believing

his master no common monk. Failure to meet the person

himself fills my heart with admiration of a mortal being.

Helpless, I return by the road leading to Mount Penglai,

a boundless expanse of misty waves and rolling waters.

Immersed in pining, I climb atop the tower, to see

snowy peaks upon peaks brilliant against a boundless sea.

自由体译文：

The abbot leaves the temple

without locking the gate, and I find

a mountain boy greeting me barefooted,

whom I ask why the temple

is so secluded and solitary?

— Even if it is emptiness itself,

we do not mind. At the boy's words

I am immensely delighted, believing

his master no common monk.

Failure to meet the person himself

fills my heart with admiration

of a mortal being. Helpless,

I return by the road leading to

Mount Penglai, a boundless expanse

of misty waves and rolling waters.

Immersed in pining,

k Dsm 禅道文化

I climb atop the tower to see
snowy peaks upon peaks brilliant
against a boundless sea.

Translator's note:

According to the Chinese legend, Penglai Mountain, inhabited by the immortals, was an isle of eternal summer in the Bohai Sea, where wine glasses refilled themselves and magic fruits granted everlasting youth. It was said that many noted figures in history went there to seek immortality. Emperor Wudi of the Han Dynasty went there several times, and though he could not find the supernatural mountains, he ordered to name the small city there Penglai.

59

怀四明亮公

In Remembrance of My Monk-Friend Zongliang

怀四明亮公

〔唐〕贯 休

孤峰含紫烟，师住此安禅。
不下便不下，如斯太可怜。
坐侵天井黑，吟久海霞蔫。
岂觉尘埃里，干戈已十年。

In Remembrance of My Monk-Friend Zongliang

[Tang Dynasty] Guan Xiu

散体译文:

  A solitary peak is wreathed in purple mist; the master lives here for introspection. In spite of an irreversible turn for secularization, no return to lay life — adorable is such an act. Sitting in meditation from daybreak to nightfall; night poem writing until morning sea clouds scatter for a fine day. Ten years elapse where wars repeat themselves through the turmoil of rolling dust; when can I see my monk-friend?

诗体译文:

  A solitary peak is wreathed in purple mist; the master lives here for introspection. In spite of an irreversible turn for secularization, no return to lay life — adorable is such an act. Sitting in meditation from daybreak to nightfall; night poem writing until morning sea clouds scatter for a fine day. Ten years

elapse where wars repeat themselves through the turmoil
of rolling dust; when can I see my monk-friend?

自由体译文：

A solitary peak is wreathed in purple mist;

the master lives here for introspection.

In spite of an irreversible turn

for secularization, no return to lay life —

adorable is such an act.

Sitting in meditation from daybreak

to nightfall; night poem writing

until morning sea clouds scatter

for a fine day. Ten years elapse

where wars repeat themselves

through the turmoil of rolling dust;

when can I see

my monk-friend?

题雪窦禅师壁

Inscription on the Wall of a Zen Master Room at Xuedou Temple

题雪窦禅师壁

［唐］方 干

飞泉溅禅石，瓶注亦生苔。
海上山不浅，天边人自来。
长年随桧柏，独夜任风雷。
猎者闻疏磬，知师入定回。

Inscription on the Wall of a Zen Master Room at Xuedou Temple

[Tang Dynasty] Fang Gan

散体译文：

The flying spring splashes onto the stone on which he is meditating; the water in his kalasa is growing mossy. Profound is the sea-side Snowy Mountain, and people far away come out of admiration. Zen-sitting beneath pine trees from year to year; solitary night in spite of thunders and storms. When he hears musical notes sparsely produced on the stone, the hunter knows the Zen master resumes his usual state of chanting sutras.

诗体译文：

The flying spring splashes onto the stone on
which he is meditating; the water in his kalasa
is growing mossy. Profound is the sea-side Snowy Mountain,
and people far away come out of admiration.
Zen-sitting beneath pine trees from year to year; solitary night
in spite of thunders and storms. When he hears musical

notes sparsely produced on the stone, the hunter knows
the Zen master resumes his usual state of chanting sutras.

自由体译文：

The flying spring splashes onto the stone
on which he is meditating; the water
in his kalasa is growing mossy.
Profound is the sea-side Snowy Mountain,
and people far away come out of admiration.
Zen-sitting beneath pine trees
from year to year;
solitary night in spite of thunders and storms.
When he hears musical notes sparsely produced
on the stone, the hunter knows
the Zen master resumes his usual state
of chanting sutras.

贻亮上人

［唐］方　干

秋水一泓常见底，涧松千尺不生枝。
空门学佛知多少，净尽心花只有师。

贻亮上人
To Accomplished Monk Zongliang

To Accomplished Monk Zongliang

[Tang Dynasty] Fang Gan

散体译文：

Like a pool limpid with crystal autumn water, or an age-old pine tree standing straight without branching. Among crowds of Buddhist learners behind the empty door, only you refuse to relax your original intention — to attain Buddhahood.

诗体译文：

Like a pool limpid with crystal autumn water, or an age-old
pine tree standing straight without branching. Among
crowds of Buddhist learners behind the empty door, only you
refuse to relax your original intention — to attain Buddhahood.

自由体译文：

Like a pool limpid with crystal
autumn water or an age-old
pine tree standing straight
without branching.
Among crowds of Buddhist
learners behind the empty
door, only you refuse to
relax your original intention —
to attain Buddhahood.

游岳林寺

Touring Yuelin Temple

游岳林寺

［唐］方 干

投闲犹自喜，古刹剡东寻。
祇树随僧老，龙溪绕岸深。
楼高春色晚，天近日光阴。
共笑家声旧，何时解盍簪。

Touring Yuelin Temple

[Tang Dynasty] Fang Gan

散体译文：

    Self-satisfaction in simple idleness, in search of the ancient temple eastward of Shanxi River. Buddhist trees age with old monks; Dragon Creek brims with water clean and clear. A high tower lingers to face spring until sunset; heaven is approachable as it dims and darkens. Amidst talking and laughing, we bid each other adieu — when can we get together again?

诗体译文：

    Self-satisfaction in simple idleness, in search
of the ancient temple eastward of Shanxi
River. Buddhist trees age with old monks;
Dragon Creek brims with water clean and clear.
A high tower lingers to face spring until sunset;
heaven is approachable as it dims and darkens.
Amidst talking and laughing, we bid each
other adieu — when can we get together again?

Self-satisfaction in simple idleness,

in search of the ancient temple eastward

of Shanxi River. Buddhist trees

age with old monks; Dragon Creek

brims with water clean and clear.

A high tower lingers to face spring

until sunset; heaven is approachable

as it dims and darkens.

Amidst talking and laughing,

we bid each other adieu —

when can we get

together again?

洗钵潭
Pool of Alms Bowl Washing

洗钵潭

[唐] 邢允中

潭水澄初地，长为洗钵供。
已能降虎豹，不问揽鱼龙。
溅沫溪莎碧，疏流石濑重。
此中清净理，继迹有禅宗。

Pool of Alms Bowl Washing

[Tang Dynasty] Xing Yunzhong

散体译文：

The temple pool water is clear and clean, a supply for washing the alms bowl. With supernatural power, it can subdue tigers and leopards and tame the dragon-fish monster. Creekside sedge is green and greener in the foam, frothing and splashing; slow rushing of water on stone after stone. Here purity and quietude reigns, when Zen Buddhism lasts — and continues.

诗体译文：

The temple pool water is clear and clean, a
supply for washing the alms bowl. With supernatural power, it can subdue tigers and leopards
and tame the dragon-fish monster. Creekside sedge
is green and greener in the foam, frothing
and splashing; slow rushing of water on stone
after stone. Here purity and quietude reigns,
when Zen Buddhism lasts — and continues.

The temple pool water is clear and clean,

a supply for washing the alms bowl.

With supernatural power, it can subdue

tigers and leopards and tame

the dragon-fish monster. Creekside sedge

is green and greener in the foam,

frothing and splashing; slow rushing

of water on stone after stone.

Here purity and quietude reigns,

when Zen Buddhism lasts —

and continues.

驻锡峰

The Buddhist Temple on the Mountaintop

驻锡峰

[唐] 邢允中

高峰常驻锡，灵异见当年。
卓立惊沙界，光辉动梵天。
鹤飞青霭外，龙护赤岚边。
丈室仍相对，重来果夙缘

The Buddhist Temple on the Mountaintop

[Tang Dynasty] Xing Yunzhong

散体译文:

The high peak houses a Buddhist temple, where the paranormal events ever thrived. Its towering posture startles the boundless universe, and Buddha's glory graces the sky of skies. Immortal cranes fly beyond the blue mist; auspicious dragons guard the mountain caught in radiant red. The room of monks is still facing the Peak of Monks; I revisit to realize my long-cherished karma.

诗体译文:

The high peak houses a Buddhist temple, where
the paranormal events ever thrived. Its towering
posture startles the boundless universe, and
Buddha's glory graces the sky of skies. Immortal
cranes fly beyond the blue mist; auspicious
dragons guard the mountain caught in radiant red.

The room of monks is still facing the Peak of Monks;

I revisit to realize my long-cherished karma.

自由体译文：

The high peak houses a Buddhist temple

where the paranormal events ever thrived.

Its towering posture startles the boundless

universe, and Buddha's glory graces

the sky of skies. Immortal cranes

fly beyond the blue mist; auspicious

dragons guard the mountain caught

in radiant red. The room of monks

is still facing the Peak of Monks; I revisit

to realize my long-cherished karma.

雪窦禅师

［唐］崔道融

雪窦峰前一派悬，雪窦五月无炎天。
客尘半日洗欲尽，师到白头林下禅。

雪窦禅师
A Zen Master at Xuedou Temple

A Zen Master at Xuedou Temple

[Tang Dynasty] Cui Daorong

散体译文:

A waterfall begins a headlong plunge against the Snowy Mountain, which witnesses no scorching heat even in summer. The lifelong worries of a visitor are washed away in half a day — what about the Zen master who lives here until he is white-crowned?

诗体译文:

A waterfall begins a headlong plunge against the Snowy
Mountain, which witnesses no scorching heat even in summer.
The lifelong worries of a visitor are washed away in half a day —
what about the Zen master who lives here until he is white-crowned?

自由体译文:

A waterfall begins a headlong plunge
against the Snowy Mountain,
which witnesses no scorching heat
even in summer. The lifelong worries
of a visitor are washed away
in half a day — what about
the Zen master who lives here
until he is white-
crowned?

天童道上

［宋］王安石

村村桑柘绿浮空，春日莺啼谷口风。
二十里松行欲尽，青山捧出梵王宫。

天童道上
Along the Way to Tiantong Temple

Along the Way to Tiantong Temple

[Song Dynasty] Wang Anshi

散体译文：

From village to village mulberry and silkworm thorn trees green the high sky; spring days see orioles twittering in the wind from the vale. Twenty miles of road fringed with pine trees come to an end, when a Buddhist palace presents itself in the depth of greener mountains.

诗体译文：

From village to village mulberry and silkworm thorn trees green
the high sky; spring days see orioles twittering in the wind from
the vale. Twenty miles of road fringed with pine trees come to an end,
when a Buddhist palace presents itself in the depth of greener mountains.

自由体译文：

From village to village mulberry
and silkworm thorn trees
green the high sky; spring days
see orioles twittering in the wind
from the vale. Twenty miles of
road fringed with pine trees come
to an end, when a Buddhist palace
presents itself in the depth
of greener mountains.

天童寺
Tiantong Temple

天童寺

[元] 金元素

喜寻方外友，特地到天童。
松径二十里，云山千万重。
倚窗僧听雪，隔岸鸟呼风。
游憩归何晚，舟行夜半钟。

Tiantong Temple

[Yuan Dynasty] Jin Yuansu

散体译文:

To seek company of a friend detached from mortal dust, I betake myself to Tiantong Temple, bright and breezy with an aura of happiness around me. The path, choked with pines, meanders for twenty miles through mountains upon mountains, a coil of mist swirling over dales and vales. My monk-friend lends an ear to the silently falling snow and, opposite the bank, birds are chirping in the wind. Late return: self-abandonment to sightseeing from a pleasure journey, until the boat is poling amidst the tolling of a midnight bell.

诗体译文:

To seek company of a friend detached from mortal dust, I betake myself to Tiantong Temple, bright and breezy with an aura of happiness around me. The path, choked with pines, meanders for twenty miles through mountains upon mountains, a coil of mist swirling over dales and vales. My monk-friend lends an ear to the silently falling snow and, opposite the bank, birds are chirping

in the wind. Late return: self-abandonment to sightseeing from a
pleasure journey, until the boat is poling amidst the tolling of a midnight
bell.

自由体译文:

To seek company of a friend detached from
mortal dust, I betake myself to Tiantong Temple,
bright and breezy with an aura of happiness
around me. The path, choked with pines, meanders
for twenty miles through mountains upon
mountains, a coil of mist swirling over
dales and vales. My monk-friend lends
an ear to the silently falling snow and,
opposite the bank, birds are chirping
in the wind. Late return: self-abandonment
to sightseeing from a pleasure journey,
until the boat is poling amidst
the tolling of a midnight bell.

杖锡道中用张宪使韵

On the Way to Zhangxi Mountain

杖锡道中用张宪使韵

〔明〕王阳明

山鸟欢呼欲问名，山花含笑似相迎。
风回碧树秋声早，雨过丹岩夕照明。
雪岭插天开玉帐，云溪环碧抱金城
悬灯夜宿茅堂静，洞鹤林僧相对清。

On the Way to Zhangxi Mountain

[Ming Dynasty] Wang Yangming

散体译文：

Mountain birds are boisterously twittering and saluting, as if asking about my name; mountain flowers are beaming with smiles, as if greeting pleasantly. The wind lingers in green trees when autumn sound is still early; the rain sprinkles over crimson rocks which are illuminated by the slanting sun. The snowy peaks piece the sky as if to open the military tent of jade, and the cloudy creeks are nursing green water gurgling about the golden city which is impregnable. A lamp is hanging in the yard of the temple where silence reigns, and quietude graces the cave cranes and forest monks.

诗体译文：

Mountain birds are boisterously twittering and saluting, as if asking about
   my name; mountain flowers are beaming with smiles, as if greeting
pleasantly.
   The wind lingers in green trees when autumn sound is still early; the rain
   sprinkles over crimson rocks which are illuminated by the slanting sun.

The snowy peaks piece the sky as if to open the military tent of jade, and the cloudy creeks are nursing green water gurgling about the golden city which is impregnable. A lamp is hanging in the yard of the temple where silence reigns, and quietude graces the cave cranes and forest monks.

自由体译文：

Mountain birds are boisterously twittering
and saluting, as if asking about my name;
mountain flowers are beaming with smiles,
as if greeting pleasantly. The wind lingers
in green trees when autumn sound is still early;
the rain sprinkles over crimson rocks
which are illuminated by the slanting sun.
The snowy peaks piece the sky as if
to open the military tent of jade,
and the cloudy creeks are nursing
green water gurgling about
the golden city which is impregnable.
A lamp is hanging in the yard of the temple
where silence reigns, and quietude
graces the cave cranes and forest monks.

少司马范公邀游溪隐二首

[明] 余 寅

查杳知何处，飘飘不自持。
精神因地别，耳目恨来迟。
莽荡千峰出，虚空万象披。
晚来岚气合，不辨有推移。

窟宅俨仙真，云霞亦是尘。
山川劳起伏，日月借嶙峋。
大海遥光起，高空爽气新。
薄寒犹户牖，清梦满松筠。

少司马范公邀游溪隐二首
Two Poems on Being Invited to Tour the Mountain Villa Xiyin

Two Poems on Being Invited to Tour the Mountain Villa Xiyin

[Ming Dynasty] Yu Yin

散体译文：

Remote and secluded, where? Swaying slowly and flowing freely, I cannot contain myself. Alteration takes place in different places according as human minds alter, and it is regretful for me to be belated in feasting my eyes on the scenery here. Thousands of aiguilles raise themselves from the enveloping sheet of vastness, when the empty air is exhibiting myriads of images and aspects. The overflowing mist gathers at the close of the day, and indiscernible is the movement.

The dens seem to be the abode of immortals, where rosy twilight and clouds are motes of dust. Hills and rills do not spare their efforts in forming elevation or depression, when the sun and the moon laboriously shine on rugged roads and cragged terrains. The vast sea embraces a remote beam of light on the rising, when the high sky affords an inexhaustible supply of fresh air. A film of thin cold air is lingering at the lattice-window, when a lucid dream is filled with bamboos lovably green.

诗体译文：

Remote and secluded, where? Swaying slowly and flowing
freely, I cannot contain myself. Alteration takes place in
different places according as human minds alter, and it is
regretful for me to be belated in feasting my eyes on the scenery
here. Thousands of aiguilles raise themselves from the enveloping sheet of vastness, when the empty air is exhibiting myriads
of images and aspects. The overflowing mist gathers

at the close of the day, and indiscernible is the movement.

The dens seem to be the abode of immortals, where rosy
twilight and clouds are motes of dust. Hills and rills do not spare
their efforts in forming elevation or depression, when the sun and
the moon laboriously shine on rugged roads and cragged terrains.
The vast sea embraces a remote beam of light on the rising,
when the high sky affords an inexhaustible supply of fresh air.
A film of thin cold air is lingering at the lattice-window, when
a lucid dream is filled with bamboos lovably green.

自由体译文:

Remote and secluded, where?
Swaying slowly and flowing freely,
I cannot contain myself. Alteration
takes place in different places
according as human minds alter,
and it is regretful for me to be belated
in feasting my eyes on the scenery here.
Thousands of aiguilles raise themselves
from the enveloping sheet of vastness,
when the empty air is exhibiting myriads
of images and aspects. The overflowing
mist gathers at the close of the day,
and indiscernible is the movement.

The dens seem to be the abode
of immortals, where rosy twilight
and clouds are motes of dust.
Hills and rills do not spare
their efforts in forming elevation
or depression, when the sun and
the moon laboriously shine on
rugged roads and cragged terrains.
The vast sea embraces a remote
beam of light on the rising, when
the high sky affords an inexhaustible
supply of fresh air. A film of thin
cold air is lingering at the lattice-
window, when a lucid dream
is filled with bamboos
 lovably green.

风土佳物

Climate & Produce

送寇侍御司马之明州

To My Friend Mr. Kou to Mingzhou

送寇侍御司马之明州

[唐] 武元衡

斗酒上河梁，惊魂去越乡。
地穷沧海阔，云入剡山长。
莲唱蒲鱼熟，人烟橘柚香。
兰亭应驻楫，今古共风光。

To My Friend Mr. Kou to Mingzhou

[Tang Dynasty] Wu Yuanheng

散体译文：

Startled by the news you are traveling to a remote place for work and stay, I prepare a farewell feast for you. At the edge of the land lies a great expanse of boundless water, and your journey is graced by Mount Shan, a cloud-veiled mountain — an enthraller, thriller, and baffler. Fishes delight in lotus ditties as oranges and shaddocks are abundant with signs of human habitation. Midway by the Orchid Pavilion, it is advisable you leave your boat and go ashore, to feast your eyes on the wonder, an age-old fair view.

诗体译文：

Startled by the news you are traveling to a remote place for work
and stay, I prepare a farewell feast for you. At the edge of the land
lies a great expanse of boundless water, and your journey
is graced by Mount Shan, a cloud-veiled mountain — an enthraller,
thriller, and baffler. Fishes delight in lotus ditties as oranges and
shaddocks are abundant with signs of human habitation. Midway

93

by the Orchid Pavilion, it is advisable you leave your boat and
go ashore, to feast your eyes on the wonder, an age-old fair view.

自由体译文：

Startled by the news you are traveling

to a remote place for work and stay,

I prepare a farewell feast for you.

At the edge of the land lies

a great expanse of boundless water,

and your journey is graced by Mount Shan,

a cloud-veiled mountain —

an enthraller, thriller, and baffler.

Fishes delight in lotus ditties as

oranges and shaddocks are abundant

with signs of human habitation.

Midway by the Orchid Pavilion,

it is advisable you leave your boat

and go ashore, to feast your eyes

on the wonder, an age-old

fair view.

Translator's note:

Mingzhou, nowadays Ningbo, a coastal city of Zhejiang Province.

寄明州于驸马使君三绝句（其一）

［唐］白居易

有花有酒有笙歌，其奈难逢亲故何。
近海饶风春足雨，白须太守闷时多。

寄明州于驸马使君三绝句（其一）
To My Friend Yu Jiyou in Mingzhou (the 1st of three poems)

To My Friend Yu Jiyou in Mingzhou (the 1st of three poems)

[Tang Dynasty] Bai Juyi

散体译文：

As the governor of Mingzhou, you do not lack beauties, mellow wines, or merriment; the only pity is that a secluded place keeps you from your relatives and friends. The fair seaside place is abundant with spring shower and spring breeze, yet I believe it is also foul with occasional tediousness.

诗体译文：

As the governor of Mingzhou, you do not lack beauties, mellow wines,

or merriment; the only pity is that a secluded place keeps you from

your relatives and friends. The fair seaside place is abundant with spring

shower and spring breeze, yet I believe, it is also foul with occasional

tediousness.

自由体译文：

As the governor of Mingzhou, you

do not lack beauties, mellow wines,

or merriment; the only pity

is that a secluded place keeps you

from your relatives and friends.

The fair seaside place is abundant with

spring shower and spring breeze,

yet I believe it is also foul

with occasional tediousness.

寄明州于驸马使君三绝句（其二）

To My Friend Yu Jiyou in Mingzhou (the 2nd of three poems)

寄明州于驸马使君三绝句（其二）

[唐] 白居易

平阳音乐随都尉，留滞三年在浙东。
吴越声邪无法用，莫教偷入管弦中。

To My Friend Yu Jiyou in Mingzhou (the 2nd of three poems)

[Tang Dynasty] Bai Juyi

散体译文：

The melody and courtesan girls ever please you as you wander about, and in the past three years they stay with you in Mingzhou, in the east of Zhejiang Province. The tune here sounds less superior to that of the Central Plains where you are from, and it takes care to guard against the purity of the Central tone.

诗体译文：

The melody and courtesan girls ever please you as you wander about, and

in the past three years they stay with you in Mingzhou, in the east of Zhejiang

Province. The tune here sounds less superior to that of the Central Plains where

you are from, and it takes care to guard against the purity of the Central tone.

白话体译文：

The melody and courtesan girls ever

please you as you wander about,

and in the past three years

they stay with you in Mingzhou,

in the east of Zhejiang Province.

The tune here sounds less superior

to that of the Central Plains

where you are from,

and it takes care to guard

against the purity of

the Central tone.

寄明州于驸马使君三绝句（其三）

〔唐〕白居易

何郎小妓歌喉好，严老呼为一串珠。
海味腥咸损声气，听看犹得断肠无。

寄明州于驸马使君三绝句（其三）
To My Friend Yu Jiyou in Mingzhou (the 3rd of three poems)

To My Friend Yu Jiyou in Mingzhou (the 3rd of three poems)

[Tang Dynasty] Bai Juyi

散体译文：

You have a young courtesan girl who boasts a melodious voice which seems to produce a string of beads in the course of her sweet singing. Now she follows you to seaside Mingzhou, which is heavily salty — in such an atmosphere, can she retain her enchanting voice?

诗体译文：

You have a young courtesan girl who boasts a melodious voice which seems to produce a string of beads in the course of her sweet singing. Now she follows you to seaside Mingzhou, which is heavily salty — in such an atmosphere, can she retain her enchanting voice?

自由体译文：

You have a young courtesan girl
who boasts a melodious voice
which seems to produce
a string of beads in the course
of her sweet singing.
Now she follows you
to seaside Mingzhou, which is
heavily salty —
in such an atmosphere,
can she retain her
enchanting voice?

秘色越器

[唐] 陆龟蒙

九秋风露越窑开，夺得千峰翠色来。
好向中宵盛沆瀣，共嵇中散斗遗杯。

秘色越器
The Greenish Blue Chinaware

The Greenish Blue Chinaware

[Tang Dynasty] Lu Guimeng

散体译文:

In the fresh late autumn wind and dew, the kiln is ready, where one piece after another piece of chinaware is glazed with various shades of green from myriads of mountains. In midnight, the china pieces can contain dew, and they vastly excel the goblet of Ji Kang as a devotee of wine.

诗体译文:

In the fresh late autumn wind and dew, the kiln is ready, where one piece
after another piece of chinaware is glazed with various shades of green
from myriads of mountains. In midnight, the china pieces can contain
dew, and they vastly excel the goblet of Ji Kang as a devotee of wine.

自由体译文:

In the fresh late autumn wind and dew,
the kiln is ready, where one piece
after another piece of chinaware is glazed
with various shades of green
from myriads of mountains.
In midnight, the china pieces
can contain dew, and they
vastly excel the goblet of
Ji Kang as a devotee
of wine.

贡余秘色茶盏

[唐] 徐夤

掠碧融青瑞色新，陶成先得贡吾君。
巧剜明月染春水，轻旋薄冰盛绿云。
古镜破苔当席上，嫩荷涵露别江濆。
中山竹叶醅初发，多病那堪中十分。

贡余秘色茶盏
The Greenish Blue Teabowls as a Tribute

The Greenish Blue Teabowls as a Tribute

[Tang Dynasty] Xu Yin

散体译文：

Ceramic glaze is made out of green like feed stock; when the chinaware is ready, it is paid as tribute to the emperor. Seemingly, the wonderful article is artfully made out of a bright full moon that brims with tea like spring water; the container looks like thin ice to hold green clouds. At a banquet, it is like an ancient round mirror whose film of moss has been broken by wiping it in the middle; again like a tender, dew-wet lotus leaf that has been plucked and taken away from the river. Tea, or clear water in it, is like nectarous wine freshly made, drinkably inviting, but I, caught by illness, can not bear to drink too much or to drink much more.

诗体译文：

Ceramic glaze is made out of green like feed stock; when the chinaware is ready,

it is paid as tribute to the emperor. Seemingly, the wonderful article is artfully made

out of a bright full moon that brims with tea like spring water; the container

looks like thin ice to hold green clouds. At a banquet, it is like an ancient round

mirror whose film of moss has been broken by wiping it in the middle; again

like a tender, dew-wet lotus leaf that has been plucked and taken away from the river. Tea, or clear water in it, is like nectarous wine freshly made, drinkably inviting,

but I, caught by illness, can not bear to drink too much or to drink much more.

自由体译文：

Ceramic glaze is made out of green like feed stock;

when the chinaware is ready, it is paid as tribute

to the emperor. Seemingly, the wonderful article

is artfully made out of a bright full moon that brims

with tea like spring water; the container looks

like thin ice to hold green clouds.

At a banquet, it is like an ancient round mirror

whose film of moss has been broken

by wiping it in the middle; again like

a tender, dew-wet lotus leaf

that has been plucked and taken away

from the river. Tea, or clear water

in it, is like nectarous wine freshly made,

drinkably inviting, but I,

caught by illness, can not bear

to drink too much or to drink much more.

寄题钱君倚明州重修众乐亭

To Governor Qian on His Renovating Joy Pavilion in Mingzhou

寄题钱君倚明州重修众乐亭

［宋］司马光

横桥通废岛，华宇出荒榛。
风月逢知己，湖山得主人。
使君如独乐，众庶必深嚬。
何以知家给，笙歌满水滨。

To Governor Qian on His Renovating Joy Pavilion in Mingzhou

[Song Dynasty] Sima Guang

散体译文：

A bridge leads to an isle that was formerly waste, and a place of hustle and bustle is made out of wilderness that was desert and desolate. The wind and the moon come into close contact with bosom friends, when lakes and mountains eventually embrace their masters. In the case of exclusive, individualistic joy, people will frown and knit their brows; in the case of invitingly inclusive joy, the waterside is thronged with a large audience immersed in chanting.

诗体译文：

A bridge leads to an isle that was formerly waste, and
a place of hustle and bustle is made out of wilderness that
was desert and desolate. The wind and the moon come into close
contact with bosom friends, when lakes and mountains
embrace their masters. In the case of exclusive,
individualistic joy, people will frown and knit

their brows; in the case of invitingly inclusive joy, the waterside is
thronged with a large audience immersed in chanting.

自由体译文：

A bridge leads to an isle

that was formerly waste,

and a place of hustle and bustle

is made out of wilderness

that was desert and desolate.

The wind and the moon come into close

contact with bosom friends,

when lakes and mountains embrace

their masters. In the case of exclusive,

individualistic joy, people will

frown and knit their brows;

in the case of invitingly inclusive

joy, the waterside is thronged

with a large audience

immersed in chanting.

观明州图

[宋] 王安石

明州城郭画中传，尚记西亭一舣船。
投老心情非复昔，当时山水故依然。

观明州图
Reading the Sketch of Mingzhou

Reading the Sketch of Mingzhou

[Song Dynasty] Wang Anshi

散体译文：

  The visage of Mingzhou is captured in the sketch, evocative of a boat used to be tethered by the Western Pavilion. Into my vale of years, my frame of mind is slightly changed, yet the hills and rills still remain as then.

诗体译文：

  The visage of Mingzhou is captured in the sketch,
  evocative of a boat used to be tethered by the Western
  Pavilion. Into my vale of years, my frame of mind is
  slightly changed, yet the hills and rills still remain as then.

自由体译文：

  The visage of Mingzhou is captured
  in the sketch, evocative of a boat
  used to be tethered
  by the Western Pavilion.
  Into my vale of years,
  my frame of mind
  is slightly changed,
  yet the hills and rills
  still remain as then.

明 州

The Affluent Lifestyle in Mingzhou

明　州

［宋］陆　游

丰年满路笑歌声，蚕麦俱收谷价平。
村步有船衔尾泊，江桥无柱架空横。
海东估客初登岸，云北山僧远入城。
风物可人吾欲住，担头莼菜正堪烹。

The Affluent Lifestyle in Mingzhou

[Song Dynasty] Lu You

散体译文：

　　A bumper year sees the road overflowing with laughter and singing; adequate silkworms and wheat and corn guarantee a moderate price. Boats are tethered at the edge of the village and in the air, a bridge spans the river. Wandering businessmen freshly go ashore from the sea as mountain monks, coming afar from beyond the clouds, enter the town. The enchanting scenery detains me to live here on; water shield to two ends of the shoulder pole makes delicious dishes.

诗体译文：

　　A bumper year sees the road overflowing with laughter
　　and singing; adequate silkworms and wheat and corn
　　guarantee a moderate price. Boats are tethered at the edge
　　of the village and in the air, a bridge spans the river. Wandering
　　businessmen freshly go ashore from the sea as mountain
　　monks, coming afar from beyond the clouds, enter the town.

The enchanting scenery detains me to live here on; water
shield to two ends of the shoulder pole makes delicious dishes.

自由体译文:

A bumper year sees the road overflowing
with laughter and singing; adequate silkworms
and wheat and corn guarantee a moderate price.
Boats are tethered at the edge of the village
and in the air, a bridge spans the river.
Wandering businessmen freshly go ashore
from the sea as mountain monks,
coming afar from beyond the clouds,
enter the town. The enchanting scenery
detains me to live here on; water shield
to two ends of the shoulder pole
makes delicious dishes.

它山诗

［宋］楼　钥

素蜺横卧作雷吼，日射细鳞银雪光。
安得此身如白鹭，翛然终日在梅梁。

它山诗
About Tuoshan Mountain

About Tuoshan Mountain

[Song Dynasty] Lou Yao

散体译文：

A white beam of light across the ridge like a flash of thunder; under sunshine, Tuoshan Mountain is silvery with snowflakes, each like a fish scale. How can I myself be like a white aigret, entitled to the enchanting view, and not like an official-prisoner in the palace?

诗体译文：

A white beam of light across the ridge like a flash of thunder; under

sunshine, Tuoshan Mountain is silvery with snowflakes, each like

a fish scale. How can I myself be like a white aigret, entitled to

the enchanting view, and not like an official-prisoner in the palace?

自由体译文：

A white beam of light across the ridge

like a flash of thunder; under sunshine,

Tuoshan Mountain is silvery with snowflakes,

each like a fish scale. How can I myself

be like a white aigret, entitled to

the enchanting view, and not

like an official-prisoner

in the palace?

它山堰

Tuoshan Mountain Weir

它山堰

[宋] 无名氏

谁将倚天剑，斫出天河水。
倾泻落人间，合流奔至此。
六丁战海若，横筑万石垒。
波涛敛潮汐，辟易走千里。
蓄泄有堨埭，深长富源委。
支派缭村落，湖渠贯城市。
千畦藉灌溉，万井酌清沘。
伟哉霖雨功，千载流不已。

Tuoshan Mountain Weir

[Song Dynasty] Anonymous

散体译文:

　　Who is wielding a sword against the sky, cutting a riverful of water which falls plumb onto the great earth? All rills and creeks converge here. People are engaged in a fierce fight against the sea-god by building dams and weirs and heightening the banks with rocks on rocks, when waves gather tides to run for thousands of miles. In case of flood discharge, there are dams to tame or temper it; the depth and length of rivers are within human knowledge. River branches nurture and embrace bank-side villages while running through towns and cities. Thousands of acres of land are conveniently irrigated, and all the wells are welling with clear water. Oh, great is the achievement in water engineering, which runs endlessly like the endlessly running water.

诗体译文：

> Who is wielding a sword against the sky, cutting
> a riverful of water which falls plumb onto the
> great earth? All rills and creeks converge here.
> People are engaged in a fierce fight against
> the sea-god by building dams and weirs and
> heightening the banks with rocks on rocks, when
> waves gather tides to run for thousands of miles.
> In case of flood discharge, there are dams to
> tame or temper it; the depth and length of rivers
> are within human knowledge. River branches
> nurture and embrace bank-side villages while
> running through towns and cities. Thousands of
> acres of land are conveniently irrigated, and all
> the wells are welling with clear water. Oh, great
> is the achievement in water engineering, which
> runs endlessly like the endlessly running water.

自由体译文：

> Who is wielding a sword against the sky,
> cutting a riverful of water which falls plumb
> onto the great earth? All rills and creeks
> converge here. People are engaged
> in a fierce fight against the sea-god
> by building dams and weirs and heightening the banks
> with rocks on rocks, when waves
> gather tides to run for thousands of miles.
> In case of flood discharge, there are dams

to tame or temper it; the depth and length

of rivers are within human knowledge.

River branches nurture and embrace

bank-side villages while running

through towns and cities.

Thousands of acres of land are conveniently irrigated

and all the wells are welling with clear water.

Oh, great is the achievement in water

engineering, which runs endlessly

like the endlessly running

water.

秋夜有怀明州张子渊

[元] 迺　贤

云表铜盘挹露华，高城凉冷咽清笳。
弓刀夜月三千骑，灯火秋风十万家。
梦断佳人弹锦瑟，酒醒童子汲冰花。
起看归路银河近，愿借张骞八月槎。

秋夜有怀明州张子渊

Missing Zhang Ziyuan of Mingzhou on an Autumn Night

Missing Zhang Ziyuan of Mingzhou on an Autumn Night

[Yuan Dynasty] Nai Xian

散体译文：

Both the memorial to the throne and the copper basin are exposed to the clear moonlight; the tall city gate tower is chilly, choked in northern reedy music. Three thousand horsemen with bows and swords gallop under the cover of moonlit night, passing by myriads of dimly-lit houses blown in autumn wind. In my fond dreams beauties are playing zither to entertain; awake from a drunken sleep, a boy is toying with ice flowers. On homeward way, when I rise to measure it in my mind, the Silver River is approachable; how I wish to take the boat of Zhang Qian, the distinguished envoy to the Western Regions where I am now, as an annual commuter between the Silver River and the boundless sea where we have been together.

诗体译文：

Both the memorial to the throne and the copper basin are exposed
to the clear moonlight; the tall city gate tower is chilly, choked in northern
reedy music. Three thousand horsemen with bows and swords gallop
under the cover of moonlit night, passing by myriads of dimly-lit houses
blown in autumn wind. In my fond dreams beauties are playing zither
to entertain; awake from a drunken sleep, a boy is toying with ice flowers.
On homeward way, when I rise to measure it in my mind, the Silver River
is approachable; how I wish to take the boat of Zhang Qian, the
distinguished
envoy to the Western Regions where I am now, as an annual commuter
between the Silver River and the boundless sea where we have been
together.

自由体译文：

Both the memorial to the throne

and the copper basin are exposed

to the clear moonlight;

the tall city gate tower is chilly,

choked in northern reedy music.

Three thousand horsemen with bows and swords

gallop under the cover of moonlit night,

passing myriads of dimly-lit houses

blown in autumn wind.

In my fond dreams beauties

are playing zither to entertain;

awake from a drunken sleep,

a boy is toying with ice flowers.

On homeward way, when I rise

to measure it in my mind,

the Silver River is approachable;

how I wish to take the boat of Zhang Qian,

the distinguished envoy to the Western Regions

where I am now, as an annual commuter

between the Silver River and the boundless sea

where we have been together.

登明州郡城楼

On the City Gate Tower of Mingzhou

登明州郡城楼

[明] 沈明臣

缥渺高楼倚日曛，万山寒色大江分。

横天中断疑为雨，截海东来半是云。

老尉亭侵龙女庙，官奴城对鲍郎坟。

登临细数前朝事，谓有黄晟领冠军。

On the City Gate Tower of Mingzhou

[Ming Dynasty] Shen Mingchen

散体译文:

The high-rise tower rises heavenward, bathed in the heat of the sun; the cold tints of myriads of hills are shared by the great river. The sky is broken in the middle, which threatens with rain; masses of clouds are surging and rolling here from the sea. The Governor-Pavilion is connected with the Dragon-Girl Temple; the town of Official-Slaves faces the tomb of Bao Gai, a sea-god worshipped by local people. Lost, on the city-gate tower of Mingzhou, in contemplation about remote past events, Governor Huang Sheng is unrivaled in political achievements.

诗体译文:

The high-rise tower rises heavenward, bathed in the heat of the sun;
the cold tints of myriads of hills are shared by the great river. The sky
is broken in the middle, which threatens with rain; masses of clouds
are surging and rolling here from the sea. The Governor-Pavilion is
connected with the Dragon-Girl Temple; the town of Official-Slaves

faces the tomb of Bao Gai, a sea-god worshipped by local people. Lost, on the city-gate tower of Mingzhou, in contemplation about remote past events, Governor Huang Sheng is unrivaled in political achievements.

自由体译文：

The high-rise tower rises heavenward,

bathed in the heat of the sun;

the cold tints of myriads of hills are shared

by the great river. The sky is broken

in the middle, which threatens with rain;

masses of clouds are surging and rolling here

from the sea. The Governor-Pavilion

is connected with the Dragon-Girl Temple;

the town of Official-Slaves faces the tomb

of Bao Gai, a sea-god worshipped by local people.

Lost on the city-gate tower of Mingzhou, in contemplation

about remote past events, Governor Huang Sheng

is unrivaled in political achievements.

四明洞天土物诗·赤堇山堇

About Local Produce of All-Luminosity Mountain: To Alpine Violet of Chijin Mountain

四明洞天土物诗·赤堇山堇

[清] 全祖望

礼经养老物，濯濯柔枝新。
冬葵与夏堇，接叶夸兼珍。
在昔欧冶子，亦豫尝真醇。
阿谁讹传讹，曾参乃杀人。

About Local Produce of All-Luminosity Mountain: To Alpine Violet of Chijin Mountain

[Qing Dynasty] Quan Zuwang

散体译文：

In the Rites it is healthy for the aged; freshly green are the tender sprouts. Winter mallow and summer viola are leafy as a rarity. Ou Yezi, a distinguished swordsmith during the Spring and Autumn Period, has taken delight in tasting it. When what is incorrect is time and again spread incorrectly, the mother of Zeng Shen is led into believing her innocent son killing a person.

诗体译文：

In the Rites it is healthy for the aged; freshly green
are the tender sprouts. Winter mallow and summer viola
are leafy as a rarity. Ou Yezi, a distinguished swordsmith
during the Spring and Autumn Period, has taken delight
in tasting it. When what is incorrect is time and again
spread incorrectly, the mother of Zeng Shen is led
into believing her innocent son killing a person.

自由体译文:

In the Rites it is healthy for the aged;
freshly green are the tender sprouts.
Winter mallow and summer viola
are leafy as a rarity.
Ou Yezi, a distinguished
swordsmith during the Spring
and Autumn Period, has taken
delight in tasting it. When what
is incorrect is time and again
spread incorrectly, the mother
of Zeng Shen is led into
believing her innocent son
killing a person.

罗汉豆
Horse Beans

罗汉豆

[清] 孙事伦

俱那八百众，儿居震旦国。
时时多化身，变幻不可测。
忽来南山下，遍布千万亿。
莹然远尘根，粉碎浑空色。
倘具大慈悲，普济人间食。

Horse Beans

[Qing Dynasty] Sun Shilun

散体译文：

Like eight hundred Buddhist arhats, horse beans grow in China. From time to time there are reincarnations, which are changing unpredictably. Later they come to the foot of the Southern Mountain, to be propagated in billions. Fresh and crystal-green, they are far from the mortal coil; when fully grown, horse beans are milled into flour for food. To Buddha's great mercy, they allay hunger of the worldlings.

诗体译文：

Like eight hundred Buddhist arhats,
horse beans grow in China. From time
to time there are reincarnations, which
are changing unpredictably. Later they
come to the foot of the Southern Mountain,

to be propagated in billions. Fresh and
crystal-green, they are far from the mortal
coil; when fully grown, horse beans are
milled into flour for food. To Buddha's great
mercy, they allay hunger of the worldlings.

自由体译文：

Like eight hundred Buddhist
arhats, horse beans grow
in China. From time to time
there are reincarnations, which
are changing unpredictably.
Later they come to the foot
of the Southern Mountain,
to be propagated in billions.
Fresh and crystal-green, they
are far from the mortal coil;
when fully grown, horse beans
are milled into flour for food.
To Buddha's great mercy, they
allay hunger of the worldlings.

象山杂咏·带鱼

［清］倪象占

渔蓑隐隐海连天，于绾山前钓晚烟。
看取孤篷三尺雪，银光铺遍带鱼船。

象山杂咏·带鱼

Poem of Xiangshan: To the Ribbon Fish

Poem of Xiangshan: To the Ribbon Fish

[Qing Dynasty] Ni Xiangzhan

散体译文：

Dim and distant is the fishing coir raincoat against the backdrop of the boundless blue sky, and before a mountain he is angling in the evening mist. A sightly sight: his solitary awning sees a heavy blanket of snow, whose silvery light paints the fishing boat.

诗体译文：

Dim and distant is the fishing coir raincoat against the backdrop
of the boundless blue sky, and before a mountain he is angling
in the evening mist. A sightly sight: his solitary awning sees a
heavy blanket of snow, whose silvery light paints the fishing boat.

自由体译文：

Dim and distant is the fishing
coir raincoat against the backdrop
of the boundless blue sky,
and before a mountain he is
angling in the evening mist.
A sightly sight: his solitary
awning sees a heavy blanket
of snow, whose silvery light
paints the fishing boat.

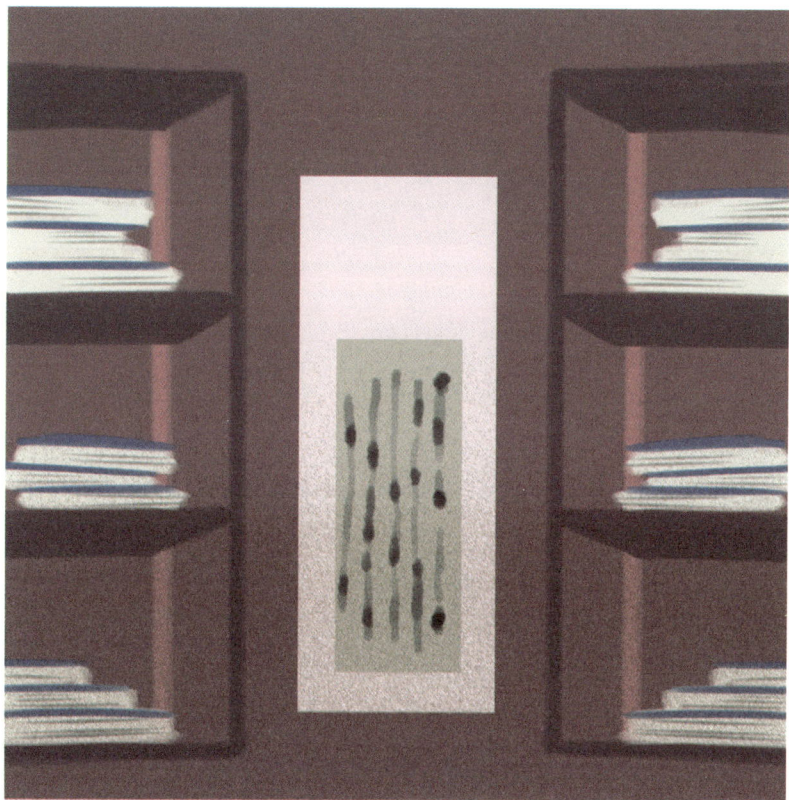

天一阁
Tianyi Pavilion Library

天一阁

［清］忻自淑

范氏传名阁，书城足巨观。

六间成奂美，一水护芒寒。

英石厨头架，香芸卷里攒。

由来规制善，藏久莫摧残。

Tianyi Pavilion Library

[Qing Dynasty] Xin Zishu

散体译文：

The fame of Tianyi Pavilion maintained by Scholar Fan Qin spreads far and wide, whose Library boasts the largest collection of books within boundaries. Six rooms, majestic and magnificent, are girdled with a cold sash-river which is constantly running. Limestone blocks are purposefully placed under the bookshelves, while the strong-scented herb is inserted within volumes, both as substance to prevent moisture or worms of the books. This long-established practice guarantees perfect preservation of books collected thither.

诗体译文：

The fame of Tianyi Pavilion of the scholar Fan Qin spreads

far and wide, whose Library boasts the largest collection

of books under heaven. Six rooms, majestic and magnificent,

are girdled with a cold sash-river which is constantly

running. Limestone blocks are purposefully placed under the

bookshelves, while the strong-scented herb is inserted
within volumes, both as substance to prevent moisture or worms
of the books. This long-established practice guarantees
perfect preservation of books collected thither.

自由体译文:

The fame of Tianyi Pavilion of the scholar Fan Qin
spreads far and wide, whose Library boasts
the largest collection of books under heaven.
Six rooms, majestic and magnificent,
are girdled with a cold sash-river
which is constantly running.
Limestone blocks are purposefully placed
under the bookshelves,
while the strong-scented herb is inserted
within volumes, both as substance to
prevent moisture or worms of the books.
This long-established practice guarantees perfect
preservation of books collected thither.

酬赠送别

Parting & Gift-presenting

送谢夷甫宰余姚县

To Mr. Xie Yifu as the County Magistrate of Yuyao

送谢夷甫宰余姚县

［唐］戴叔伦

君去方为县，兵戈尚未销。
邑中残老小，乱后少官僚。
廨宇经兵火，公田没海潮。
到时应变俗，新政满余姚。

To Mr. Xie Yifu as the County Magistrate of Yuyao

[Tang Dynasty] Dai Shulun

散体译文：

　　You depart for Yuyao as the county magistrate, where the flames of war are still flaming. In the postwar period, only the old and the weak survive; official candidates also lack. Administration houses have been burned down; public fields are immersed in seawater — no supply of food and shelter. When you assume your post, you shall implement new policies, and steps shall be taken to ameliorate the social situation.

诗体译文：

　　You depart for Yuyao as the county magistrate,
　　where the flames of war are still flaming. In the
　　postwar period, only the old and the weak survive;
　　official candidates also lack. Administration houses have
　　been burned down; public fields are immersed in
　　seawater — no supply of food and shelter. When

you assume your post, you shall implement new policies,

and steps shall be taken to ameliorate the social situation.

自由体译文：

You depart for Yuyao as the county magistrate,

where the flames of war are still flaming.

In the postwar period, only the old and the weak survive;

official candidates also lack.

Administration houses have been burned down;

public fields are immersed in seawater —

no supply of food and shelter.

When you assume your post,

you shall implement new policies

and steps shall be taken

to ameliorate the social situation.

送施肩吾东归

Farewell to Shi Jianwu

送施肩吾东归

［唐］张　籍

知君本是烟霞客，被荐因来城阙间。
世业偏临七里濑，仙游多在四明山。
早闻诗句传人遍，新得科名到处闲。
惆怅灞亭相送去，云中琪树不同攀。

Farewell to Shi Jianwu

[Tang Dynasty] Zhang Ji

散体译文：

　　You are famed to be a hermit in mist and clouds, who come to the city after being recommended. The ancestral business concentrates in Seven-Mile Rapids, and most of your free comings and leisurely goings are within the range of the All-Luminosity Mountain. You enjoy a long-standing reputation for your poems, and with an added credit you are idling about. At the Parting Pavilion, we lingeringly bid farewell to each other, for we will climb the clouds-scraping celestial trees separately.

诗体译文：

　　You are famed to be a hermit in mist and clouds, who come
　　to the city after being recommended. The ancestral business
　　concentrates in Seven-Mile Rapids, and most of your free
　　comings and leisurely goings are within the range of the Four-
　　Luminosity Mountain. You enjoy a long-standing reputation
　　for your poems, and with an added credit you are idling about.

At the Parting Pavilion, we lingeringly bid farewell to each other,

for we will climb the clouds-scraping celestial trees separately.

自由体译文：

You are famed to be a hermit in mist and clouds,

who come to the city after being recommended.

The ancestral business concentrates in Seven-Mile Rapids,

and most of your free comings and leisurely goings

are within the range of the All-Luminosity Mountain.

You enjoy a long-standing reputation for your poems,

and with an added credit you are idling about.

At the Parting Pavilion, we lingeringly bid

farewell to each other, for we will climb

the clouds-scraping celestial

trees separately.

寄宁海李明府

To County Magistrate Li of Ninghai

寄宁海李明府

[唐] 周 贺

山县风光异，公门水石清。
一官居外府，几载别东京。
故疾梅天发，新诗雪夜成。
家贫思减选，时静忆归耕。
把疏寻书义，澄心得狱情。
梦灵邀客解，剑古拣人呈。
守月通宵坐，寻花迥路行。
从来知爱道，何虑白髭生。

To County Magistrate Li of Ninghai

[Tang Dynasty] Zhou He

散体译文：

The mountain areas boast a uniquely fair scenery, and the official yard embraces limpid water with river stones. As an official in such a remote place, we will be apart for several years from Luoyang, the capital. In rainy season of drippy days, the abiding illness recurs; a poem is composed in the depths of a snowy night. Family poverty reduces my occasions to attend for screening and choosing officers; in current social stability, I will return to resume my former farming. Get to the real meaning hidden in dossier according to classics; detached from social power and worldly benefits, try to clarify the details of a case. A fond dream is open to interpretation by a visitor; an ancient sword is presented only to my bosom friend. Sitting and watching the moon throughout the night; a remote journey is taken without hesitation in search of flowers rare and fair. I know you are a constant follower of Tao, which relieves you of worries whitening your hair.

诗体译文:

The mountain areas boast a uniquely fair scenery, and
the official yard embraces limpid water with river stones.
As an official in such a remote place, we will be apart for
several years from Luoyang, the capital. In rainy season of
drippy days, the abiding illness recurs; a poem is composed
in the depths of a snowy night. Family poverty reduces my
occasions to attend for screening and choosing officers; in
current social stability, I will return to resume my former
farming. Get to the real meaning hidden in dossier according
to classics; detached from social power and worldly benefits,
try to clarify the details of a case. A fond dream is open to
interpretation by a visitor; an ancient sword is presented only
to my bosom friend. Sitting and watching the moon throughout
the night; a remote journey is taken without hesitation in search
of flowers rare and fair. I know you are a constant follower of Tao,
which relieves you of worries whitening your hair.

自由体译文:

The mountain areas boast a uniquely fair scenery,
and the official yard embraces limpid water with
river stones. As an official in such a remote place,
we will be apart for several years from Luoyang, the capital.
In rainy season of drippy days, the abiding illness

recurs; a poem is composed in the depths
of a snowy night. Family poverty reduces my occasions
to attend for screening and choosing officers;
in current social stability, I will return to resume
my former farming. Get to the real meaning hidden
in dossier according to classics; detached from
social power and worldly benefits,
try to clarify the details of a case.
A fond dream is open to interpretation
by a visitor; an ancient sword is presented
only to my bosom friend. Sitting and watching
the moon throughout the night; a remote journey
is taken without hesitation in search of flowers
rare and fair. I know you are a constant follower
of Tao, which relieves you of worries
whitening your hair.

酬余姚郑模明府见赠长句四韵

To County Magistrate Zheng Mo of Yuyao

酬余姚郑模明府见赠长句四韵

〔唐〕张　祜

仙令东来值胜游，人间稀遇一扁舟。
万重山色连江微，十里溪声到县楼。
吏隐不妨彭泽远，公才多谢武城优。
生疏莫笑沧浪叟，白首直竿是直钩。

To County Magistrate Zheng Mo of Yuyao

[Tang Dynasty] Zhang Hu

散体译文：

　　As a county magistrate, you make an eastward journey to Yuyao where I am touring pleasantly, the last place where I expect to meet you. Myriads of hills extend to the riverside; ten miles of babbling water runs all the way to the county office house. As a hermit-official, Yuyao is an ideal place to handle governmental affairs, and the local people will be thankful to you for your favorable political measures. As a new comer, please don't laugh at the riverside white-crowned fishermen, who are angling, not for fishes, but just for fun.

诗体译文：

　　As a county magistrate, you make an eastward journey to Yuyao where I am touring pleasantly, the last place where I expect to meet you. Myriads of hills extend to the riverside; ten miles of babbling water runs all the way to the county office house. As a hermit-official, Yuyao is an ideal place to handle governmental affairs, and the local people will be thankful to you for your favorable political measures. As a new comer, please don't laugh at the riverside white-crowned fishermen, who are angling, not for fishes, but just for fun.

自由体译文：

As a county magistrate, you make an eastward journey

to Yuyao where I am touring pleasantly,

the last place I expect to meet you.

Myriads of hills extend to the riverside;

ten miles of babbling water runs all the way

to the county office house. As a hermit-official,

Yuyao is an ideal place to handle governmental affairs,

and the local people will be thankful

to you for your favorable political measures.

As a new comer, please don't laugh at

the riverside white-crowned fishermen,

who are angling not for fishes,

but just for fun.

晓发鄞江北渡寄崔韩二先辈

To Two Seniors at the Northern Ferry of Yinjiang River

晓发鄞江北渡寄崔韩二先辈

[唐] 许　浑

南北信多岐，生涯半别离。

地穷山尽处，江泛水寒时。

露晓兼葭重，霜晴橘柚垂。

无劳促回楫，千里有心期。

To Two Seniors at the Northern Ferry of Yinjiang River

[Tang Dynasty] Xu Hun

散体译文：

　　Journeying northward and southward, getting together and bidding farewell make a good part of my wandering life. At the end of the mountain and at the edge of the land, the river water is overflowing with chilliness. The morning reed is reedy in dew and dewdrops; the clear frost freshens fresh oranges and shaddocks. No need for two senior friends to urge me back by boat — we enjoy a complete meeting of minds.

诗体译文：

　　Journeying northward and southward, getting together
　　and bidding farewell make a good part of my wandering
　　life. At the end of the mountain and at the edge of the land,
　　the river water is overflowing with chilliness.
　　The morning reed is reedy in dew and dewdrops;
　　the clear frost freshens fresh oranges and shaddocks.

No need for two senior friends to urge me back

by boat — we enjoy a complete meeting of minds.

自由体译文：

Journeying northward and southward,

getting together and bidding farewell

make a good part of my wandering life.

At the end of the mountain and at the edge of the land,

river water is overflowing with chilliness.

The morning reed is reedy in dew and dewdrops;

the clear frost freshens fresh oranges and shaddocks.

No need for two senior friends to urge me

back by boat — we enjoy a complete

meeting of minds.

游四明山刘樊二真人祠题山下孙氏居

Inscription on the Wall of Mr. Sun after Touring the Temple of Two Taoist Immortals in the All-Luminosity Mountain

游四明山刘樊二真人祠题山下孙氏居

〔唐〕李　频

久在仙坛下，全家是地仙。
池塘来乳洞，禾黍接芝田。
起看青山足，还倾白酒眠。
不知尘世事，双鬓逐流年。

Inscription on the Wall of Mr. Sun after Touring the Temple of Two Taoist Immortals in the All-Luminosity Mountain

[Tang Dynasty] Li Pin

散体译文：

　　Living long beneath the shrine of immortals, Mr. Sun and his family are like immortals aground. Their pond has its source from the Milky Spring, and their crops extend to the immortal field of glossy Ganoderma. Rising in morning, green hills meet the eye, which completes their happiness; returning in evening, liquor and spirits tease their lips, which conduces to sleep at ease. Excluded from social entanglement, their temple hair grows gray with the years passing by.

诗体译文：

　　Living long beneath the shrine of immortals, Mr. Sun and
　　his family are like immortals aground. Their pond has its source
　　from the Milky Spring, and their crops extend to the immortal field
　　of glossy Ganoderma. Rising in morning, green hills meet the eye,
　　which completes their happiness; returning in evening,

liquor and spirits tease their lips, which conduces to sleep at ease.

Excluded from social entanglement, their temple hair grows gray with the years passing by.

自由体译文:

Living long beneath the shrine of immortals,

Mr. Sun and his family are like immortals aground.

Their pond has its source from the Milky Spring,

and their crops extend

to the immortal field of glossy Ganoderma.

Rising in morning, green hills meet the eye,

which completes their happiness;

returning in evening, liquor and spirits tease

their lips, which conduces

to sleep at ease. Excluded from social

entanglement, their temple hair grows gray

with the years passing by.

明州江亭夜别段秀才

Night Adieu to Mr. Duan at a Riverside Pavilion of Mingzhou

明州江亭夜别段秀才

〔唐〕李　频

离亭向水开，时候复蒸梅。
霹雳灯烛灭，蒹葭风雨来。
京关虽共语，海峤不同回。
莫为莼鲈美，天涯滞尔才。

Night Adieu to Mr. Duan at a Riverside Pavilion of Mingzhou

[Tang Dynasty] Li Pin

散体译文：

　　The departing riverside pavilion is lost in a study of the river, when the rainy season sets in. A thunderstorm thunders out the candle; the riverside reed is reeling and rolling under a sudden spell of wind and rain. Verbal agreement at the city gate is broken by the seaside, where we part company in opposite directions. Delicious is your native produce, suggestive of your reluctance to be away from home, which would waste your talent. Away, away from home, to get your talent developed to the fullest.

诗体译文：

　　The departing riverside pavilion is lost in a study of the river, when the rainy season sets in. A thunderstorm thunders out the candle; the riverside reed is reeling and rolling under a sudden spell of wind and rain. Verbal agreement at the city gate is broken by the seaside, where we part company in opposite directions. Delicious is your native produce, suggestive of your reluctance to be away from home, which would waste your talent.

Away, away from home, to get your talent developed to the fullest.

自由体译文：

The departing riverside pavilion

is lost in a study of the river

when the rainy season sets in.

A thunderstorm thunders out

the candle; the riverside reed

is reeling and rolling under

a sudden spell of wind and rain.

Verbal agreement at the city gate

is broken by the seaside, where

we part company in opposite directions.

Delicious is your native produce,

suggestive of your reluctance

to be away from home, which would

waste your talent. Away, away

from home, to get your talent

developed to the fullest.

题慈溪张丞壁

To Mr. Zhang, a Subprefect-Friend of Cixi County

题慈溪张丞壁

［唐］方　干

因君贰邑蓝溪上，遣我维舟红叶时。
共向乡中非半面，俱惊鬓里有新丝。
仁看孤洁成三考，应笑愚疏舍一枝。
貌似故人心尚喜，相逢况是旧相知。

To Mr. Zhang, a Subprefect-Friend of Cixi County

[Tang Dynasty] Fang Gan

散体译文：

Assuming subprefect of Cixi County, where a crystal creek runs through, you tell me to prepare a boat in the season of red leaves. As countrymen instead of nodding acquaintances, we are mutually surprised at each other's gray hairs. Being an honest and uncorrupted official, you are expected to achieve distinguishably in a duration of three years, while I humbly choose a lower branch to perch. The meeting of friends gladdens the hearts — you and me, we are more than friends of friends.

诗体译文：

Assuming subprefect of Cixi County, where a crystal creek runs through, you tell me to prepare a boat in the season of red leaves. As countrymen instead of nodding acquaintances, we are mutually surprised at each other's gray hairs. Being an honest and uncorrupted official, you are expected to achieve distinguishably in a duration of three years, while I humbly choose a lower branch to perch. The meeting of friends gladdens the hearts — you and me, we are more than friends of friends.

自由体译文:

Assuming subprefect of Cixi County, where a crystal
creek runs through, you tell me to prepare a boat in the season
of red leaves. As countrymen instead of
nodding acquaintances, we are mutually
surprised at each other's gray hairs.
Being an honest and uncorrupted official,
you are expected to achieve distinguishably
in a duration of three years, while I humbly
choose a lower branch to perch.
The meeting of friends
gladdens the hearts — you and me,
we are more than friends
of friends.

别四明钟尚书

〔唐〕杜荀鹤

九华天际碧嵯峨，无奈春来入梦何。
难与英雄论教化，却思猿鸟共烟萝。
风前柳态闲时少，雨后花容淡处多。
都大人生有离别，且将诗句代离歌。

别四明钟尚书
Farewell to My Friend Zhong Jiwen in All-Luminosity Mountain

Farewell to My Friend Zhong Jiwen in All-Luminosity Mountain

[Tang Dynasty] Du Xunhe

散体译文：

My native Jiuhua Mountain towers into the boundlessly blue sky, and my spring dream has been bluer with its illusive and attractive form. Homesickness prevents me from joining you to collaborate efforts for a greater career, when I am infatuated with the leisurely birds and monkeys and green vegetation of the Mountain. Willowy twigs, lingering and leaning in the wind, are busy seeing people off, and spring flowers, after a shower of rain, are soaked, fallen, and faded. Human life itself is full of partings and reunions, and I compose this poem as a farewell song.

诗体译文：

My native Jiuhua Mountain towers into the boundlessly blue sky, and my spring dream has been bluer with its illusive and attractive form. Homesickness prevents me from joining you to collaborate efforts for a greater career, when I am infatuated with the leisurely birds and monkeys and green vegetation of the Mountain. Willowy twigs, lingering and leaning in the wind, are busy seeing people off, and spring flowers, after a shower of rain, are soaked, fallen, and faded. Human life itself is full of partings and reunions, and I compose this poem as a farewell song.

自由体译文：

My native Jiuhua Mountain towers
into the boundlessly blue sky,
and my spring dream has been bluer

with its illusive and attractive form.

Homesickness prevents me from joining you

to collaborate efforts for a greater career

when I am infatuated with the leisurely birds

and monkeys and green vegetation of the Mountain.

Willowy twigs, lingering and leaning in the wind,

are busy seeing people off, and spring flowers,

after a shower of rain, are soaked, fallen, and faded.

Human life itself is full of partings and reunions,

and I compose this poem

as a farewell song.

赠安富之同年归高丽（节选）

To My Friend Back to Corea (excerpt)

赠安富之同年归高丽（节选）

［宋］程端学

我家东海西，君家东海东。
总是东海上，海阔无由通。
我如海中云，君如海中龙。
云龙以类应，万里终相从。

To My Friend Back to Corea (excerpt)

[Song Dynasty] Cheng Duanxue

散体译文：

　　I live west of the East Sea and you, east of the ocean. Through the vast expanse of the East Sea, constantly, there is no easy come-and-go. I am like a piece of cloud over the sea and you, like a dragon in the ocean. When birds of a feather flock together, the flight of a dragon cannot dispense with clouds.

诗体译文：

　　I live west of the East Sea and you,
　　east of the ocean. Through the vast
　　expanse of the East Sea, constantly,
　　there is no easy come-and-go. I am
　　like a piece of cloud over the sea and
　　you, a dragon in the ocean. When birds
　　of a feather flock together, the flight
　　of a dragon cannot dispense with clouds.

白山体译文:

I live west of the East Sea

and you, east of the ocean.

Through the vast expanse of the East Sea,

constantly, there is no easy come-and-go.

I am like a piece of cloud

over the sea and you,

a dragon in the ocean.

When birds of a feather flock

together, the flight of a dragon

cannot dispense with clouds.

上元诸彦集天一阁即事

Composed at the Gathering of Friends at Tianyi Pavilion

上元诸彦集天一阁即事

[明] 范 钦

阛城花月拥笙歌，仙客何当结轸过。
吟倚鳌峰夸白雪，笑看星驾度银河。
苑风应节舒梅柳，径雾含香散绮罗。
接席呼卢堪一醉，向来心赏屡蹉跎。

Composed at the Gathering of Friends at Tianyi Pavilion

[Ming Dynasty] Fan Qin

散体译文:

Moonlit flowers and piping music fill the town — the best time for the immortal-guests to drive their wagons here in an endless stream. It is the biggest aggregation of elites and highbrows who appreciate White Snow Melody; laughing with glee, the wagons are moving across the Silver River. The seasonable spring breeze unfolds and unfurls the willows and plum trees in the garden, whose paths are foggy and fragrant with silky things. Through wine games the drunkards are still drinking, for their high aspirations have not been fulfilled.

诗体译文:

Moonlit flowers and piping music fill the town — the best time
for the immortal-guests to drive their wagons here in an endless
stream. It is the biggest aggregation of elites and highbrows who
appreciate White Snow Melody; laughing with glee, the wagons are
moving across the Silver River. The seasonable spring breeze unfolds

and unfurls the willows and plum trees in the garden, whose paths are foggy and fragrant with silky things. Through wine games the drunkards are still drinking, for their high aspirations have not been fulfilled.

自由体译文：

Moonlit flowers and piping music
fill the town — the best time
for the immortal-guests to drive
their wagons here in an endless stream.
It is the biggest aggregation of
elites and highbrows who appreciate
White Snow Melody; laughing with glee,
the wagons are moving across the Silver River.
The seasonable spring breeze unfolds
and unfurls the willows and plum trees
in the garden, whose paths are
foggy and fragrant with silky things.
Through wine games the drunkards
are still drinking, for their high
aspirations have not been fulfilled.

古代诗人喜好四处吟游，留下了数不胜数的可贵诗篇，我们读起这些诗歌仿佛也被邀请至那时那地那景，即便时隔千百余年，也能依稀触摸古人鲜活的脉搏，感受各地别样的风土人情。虽然我们无法完整仔细地回忆这座城市厚重的历史，却仍希望能够通过诗歌这一跨越古今的文化表征，与读者一同走近千百年前的宁波，在诗句的一张一弛间，在阅读的一呼一吸间，触摸它过往的情貌。

宁波古称"四明"，唐开元时有独立的行政建置，始称"明州"。唐代宁海县属于台州，余姚县属越州，但由于今天两地都属宁波，所以将相关诗歌的收录考虑在内，在唐代属明州，今不属宁波的，则不予考虑。《四明雅韵——宁波古代诗歌英译》主要参考《全唐诗》《全宋诗》《宁波地名诗》《泠泠唐音：唐诗咏宁波全解》等诗歌文献，遴选出 60 首唐、五代以降历朝吟咏宁波的诗歌，我们将搜集的诗歌分为地理山水、禅道文化、风土佳物、酬赠送别四个编目呈现，在确保诗歌审美价值的同时，也力图将宁波的古风貌、古生活更全面、立体地介绍给世界。

诗集的编选与翻译过程，既是编选团队走近宁波古风，向世界展现宁波神采的过程，也是一次跨学科、跨领域、跨地区的学术对话和智慧传递过程。眼前这部诗集从起念到定稿凝聚了很多人的心血，感谢我的好朋友中南大学文学与新闻传播学院杨雨教授，她在繁忙的工作和节目录制之余帮助查阅专业古诗词文献资源，多次在凌晨发来微信语音留言，对所选诗句的典故和意蕴进行解读与阐释；感谢宁波大学人文与传媒学院李亮伟教授在文集即将定稿阶段依然细致、耐心地帮助调整编目并指导遴选替换 7 首跟宁波弱相关的诗篇、审定版本差异造成的异体字；感谢中国外文局前副局长黄友义先生对整个编选翻译团队的肯定和鼓励，感谢他拨冗帮助审定英文书名并转来资深外国翻译家的意见；感谢南开大学张智中教授的执笔翻译，他对中英诗歌的高深造诣，直接决定了整个团队对外讲好宁波诗歌故事的质量和方向；感谢宁波出版社袁志坚总编、越秀外国语学院陈科芳教授在翻译定编过程中的答疑解惑；感谢远在故乡大运河畔的挚友桑莹女士用秋日古栗园的图片解答团队解读唐人于季友《范处士在育王寺书碑因以寄赠》诗中"遥知松径望，栗叶满山红"意境时的困难……

诗歌是我国文化的瑰宝，幸运的是，即便时过境迁，我们仍能从诗歌的呼吸中，感受千百年来宁波的诗意与温度。在宁波与世界积极对话的当下，阅读这些诗歌，正是解码宁波过往与当下，用诗意的方式了悟宁波美好明天的过程，在此，我们不揣冒昧奉上双语插画版本，期盼与各位共度一段美好的阅读时光。

辛红娟

壬寅年桃月于宁波大学

Chinese poets in ancient times are fond of traveling while composing poems, leaving to us a great wealth of literary pieces by which, while reading, we are unconsciously brought back to the then very scene where these vignettes were written, in spite of the space of over one thousand years — we can still feel the strong pulse of ancient people and get ourselves acquainted with the various customs through the length and breadth of China. Ningbo is a city with historical deposits which defy our detailed description here, and we resort to poetry about the city as the cultural representation through different ages, so as to get, together with readers, closer to Ningbo which manifests itself as it was during the past one thousand years — through lines short and long, along with our chest heaving with each breath upon reading these breathtaking pieces.

Ningbo was known as "Siming" in ancient China and, during the Kaiyuan Period (713—741) of the Tang Dynasty (618—907), it was subjected to an independent administrative regionalization under the name of Mingzhou. During the Tang Dynasty, Ninghai County was under the administration of Taizhou, Yuyao County under that of Yuezhou, and today the two places are under the governance of Ningbo, hence poems about the two places are collected in the book; as for those places under Mingzhou during the Tang Dynasty but nowadays beyond the domain of Ningbo, the relevant poems are dispensed with. The source of *Poems Portraying Centuries-old City of Ningbo* is mainly from Chinese poetry books such as *The Complete Poetry of Tang Dynasty*, *The Complete Poetry of Song Dynasty*, *Poetry About Place Names of Ningbo*, *Interpretation of the Best Tang Poems About Ningbo*, etc. Altogether 60 poems since the Tang Dynasty and the Five Dynasties portraying Ningbo are included in this book, which are categorized into "Hills & Rills", "Zenism & Daoism", "Climate & Produce", and "Parting & Gift-presenting", through which, while exhibiting the aesthetic value of poetry, attempt has been made to introduce Ningbo as we read it, including its

177

ancient scenes of life, to the world.

The compilation and translation of this poetry anthology is both a process of the team's approaching the ancient lifestyle of Ningbo with the aim of exhibiting its charm to the world and a process of academic dialogue and wisdom sharing which is interdisciplinary, trans-field, and trans-regional. From its germination to completion, this poetry anthology embodies the painstaking efforts of a host of people, and my indebtedness goes first to my close friend Yang Yu, professor of the School of Literature and Journalism of Central South University, who spares time out of her tight schedule of busy daily work and TV show making to explain the phrases and literary allusions in the poems, sometimes in the wee hours, besides consulting ancient poetry books or relevant resources. And my indebtedness also goes to Li Liangwei, professor of the School of Journalism and Communication of Ningbo University, who carefully and conscientiously assists in arranging the contents even toward the close of the compilation, in addition to replacing 7 weakly Ningbo-related poems with those which are more closely connected with the city of Ningbo and deciding the variant Chinese characters owing to different existing Chinese versions; to Huang Youyi, former vice director of China Foreign Languages Publishing Administration, who has warmly encouraged the team of the book while giving advice for the English name of the book and providing suggestions given by overseas senior translators; to Zhang Zhizhong, professor of Nankai University, who undertakes the translation and, owing to his knowledge in Chinese and English poetry, has guaranteed the high-quality rendering of the poems; to Yuan Zhijian, general editor of Ningbo Press as well as to Chen Kefang, professor of Zhejiang Yuexiu University, who have answered some questions in the course of compiling and translating; and to my bosom friend Ms. Sang Ying who, living by the Grand Canal of my hometown, has deciphered with picture the baffling line of "looking along the path lined with pines, the mountain is flamboyant with flickering chestnut trees" from Fan Di's *Inscription on the Stone Tablet at Ashoka Temple*, a poem by the Tang Dynasty poet Yu Jiyou.

Poetry is the cultural treasure of China and, as luck would have it, we can still feel the poetic warmth of Ningbo which runs through over one thousand years, in spite of the great changes of things. At present, Ningbo is actively engaged in dialogue with the world, and reading poems in this book is the means to decode Ningbo, both as it is and as it was, as well as a poetic way to look into the bright future of Ningbo. Hence this bilingual illustrated poetry anthology for your delightful reading, hopefully.

Xin Hongjuan

April, 2022

Ningbo University